Darkness & Good

Science Fiction and Fantasy Short Stories

LIANA BROOKS
AMY LAURENS

Darkness & Good

Science Fiction and Fantasy
Short Stories

LIANA BROOKS
AMY LAURENS

AUSTRALIA

ISBN-13: 978-1-925825-99-2

www.inkprintpress.com

National Library of Australia Cataloguing-in-Publication Data
Laurens, Amy 1985 –
Darkness and Good : Science Fiction and Fantasy Short Stories
        274 p.
        ISBN-13: 978-1-925825-99-2
        Inkprint Press, Canberra, Australia
        1. Anthologies 2. Fantasy fiction 3. Science fiction 4.
        Short stories.
        Brooks, Liana, author.

Summary: Dark and humorous fantasy and science fiction short stories.
Includes illustrations.

First Edition: March 2017
Printed in the United States of America.

Cover design © Amy Laurens.
Interior art © Amy Laurens.

INTRODUCTION

It's December 2013. Amy has not long finished reading *The Curiosities*, a collection of short stories by Maggie Stiefvater, Tessa Gratton and Brenna Yovanoff. It's been a couple of years since she was able to write fiction, mostly due to postnatal depression, and having just completed the first draft of a non-fiction worldbuilding book, she's keen to get back into the swing of fictional things: a continuing short story challenge sounds like just the thing.

It's January 2016. Liana notes on Twitter that "if @InkyLaurens suggests a 'small and simple plan' please realise you've just committed to a ten-year plot". This book is the result of one of those plots: instead of being just a fun story challenge to get Amy back in the swing of writing fiction, the *Darkness and Good* blog was born: a place for (mostly) weekly, (usually) unedited short fiction. Some of it's dark, hopefully it's at least passably good, but regardless it's grown its own little readership and become something a lot grander than Amy ever envisaged.

That happens a lot.

It's March 2017, or later: you're holding this book in your hands, and we owe you our thanks. We've edited these stories (some more than others) and written some new ones, and we hope the end result makes you *feel*. If it does, please consider leaving a review—but regardless, thank you, amazing reader, for making this journey possible.

CONTENTS

THE BOY NAMED NO
Liana Brooks

TWO STRAIGHT LINES OF unwanted waifs stood at military attention by their cots. Matron L. R. Rus' heels clicked as she marched down the rows, inspecting hospital corners, checking under the beds for debris, ordering hands held out so she could verify they were properly scrubbed.

The last cot stood alone, blankets folded at the end of the bed where the orderly had placed them the night before. The cot's tow-headed owner was missing.

Again.

Matron Rus scowled. "Justice Saber Rus, get out here this instant!" Not expecting much, she checked under the bed. Nothing. A twinge of clan pride kept her from screaming. He was a Rus; even if he was unwanted, at least he was intelligent.

She eyed his footlocker, then, with practiced ease, overrode his lock code. Shredded uniforms and a shredded gray bag.

Frustration boiling over, she turned to the boy across the aisle. "Where is Justice?"

"He left last night, ma'am."

She scrolled through her mental list of names, trying to place the dark-haired child. Virtuous Shield Pantros. Age six, large for his age and clan. Probably not a full Pantros. "Why, Mister Shield, did you not inform anyone when Justice left?"

"We were told not to make any noise, ma'am." His dark brown gaze slid upward, watching her.

"You didn't consider the consequences of allowing him to wander away?"

"I did, ma'am. But I can't break the rules, ma'am," he said with infuriating calm.

Matron Rus smiled. "Rebellion by obedience, how very charming. Unit!" she bellowed. "Move out to the cafeteria. You will be fed when Mister Saber joins you."

The children marched out.

With a sigh, Matron Rus collected the tattered gray duffel and dropped it in the carbon recycler. It was always the first thing he destroyed when he threw a tantrum.

She opened the hall closet, looking for a replacement.

"Matron Laura?" a voice interrupted.

"Yes?"

Terssa Camlin Fisher stepped around the corner. "Unit Five just arrived in the kitchen and the little Rondros Pantros girl told me they were waiting for Justice. Where is he?"

"A very good question, Miss Camlin. He's run off again."

Terssa sighed. "The poor dear. He was so upset when the claims list came in yesterday and he wasn't on it."

"He'll never be on the claims list. He's been here for six years and his name has never been listed."

"Little Erinna Sandol Rus was listed this year, and she's nearly nine."

"Erinna's mother brought her to the crèche. The enforcers found Justice wrapped in a bag in a trash can." She slammed the closet door. "Children found in trash cans are not later claimed by their ecstatic family. Now, where are the gray duffels?"

"W-We're out. I can put in an order for more."

Matron Rus grumbled and opened the closet again. "No matter. If the boy didn't shred his things every time he was upset, he wouldn't need a new bag." She pulled out a navy blue bag meant for the children two years younger than Justice. Each year group had their own color, a simple strategy to help the children find their things. Writing names on the inside was the other half of the strategy, and the major sticking point for the little Rus boy.

"I'm going to wait for Justice. Keep an eye on the other children. They'll have to sleep in the cafeteria tonight. I don't want one of his cohorts smuggling him food."

"Yes, Matron."

She returned to the room, lost in thought. *If I were a six-year-old boy, where would I hide?*

Fan-shaped leaves rapping the windowsill drew her attention. The Aral mountains rose in the distance. Thick copses of pine, snow in high summer, and bitter cold tarns. Yes. That would tempt a boy away as the frost cleared from the grass.

Matron Rus took a seat on the boy's spotless footlocker and waited.

Early morning light brightened to noon. Noon warmth faded into early evening. Cold wind rushed down from the mountain heights. As the supper bell rang, she saw one shadow moving amid the lengthening shadows of the trees.

Over the windowsill two white ears appeared. A furry white face with distinctive black stripes followed. Ice-blue eyes glared and whiskers twitched.

Matron Rus stood up and brushed imaginary dust off her skirt. "Well, Mister Saber. Have you finally decided to grace the house with your presence?" She heard his stomach growl.

The little white tiger cub slunk over the windowsill, green burrs clinging to him. Blood matted the fur on his left leg.

"Playing rough were we, Mister Saber?"

Justice sat down in front of her and deliberately licked his paw as if to say she had no control over him.

"Stand up, Mister Saber. I demand an accounting."

The pale blue eyes narrowed. The cub straightened, shoulders arching back. He sat tall and kept growing taller, stretching and flowing out of the white tiger's form and into that of a chubby-cheeked blond boy with dark tan skin and ice-blue eyes.

The burrs fell to the floor with a papery whisper.

"Give me your hand," the matron ordered. He held out his left hand for inspection. "Neatly done. Why didn't you shift the injury away before you came in?"

"Didn't wanna," the boy whispered, his voice rasping.

"Hmmmm. Turn." She inspected him head to toe as he pivoted. "No other signs of injury." Although his ribs were showing. "How many times a week are you shifting?"

He shrugged. "Lots."

"You need to eat more if you are changing forms on a regular basis, Justice. If you are shifting more than once or twice a week, I need to know." Her heart bled for the pathetic little boy. Unwanted. Unheeded. And, may the ancestors forgive her, so unlovable. Prickly as an urchin. There were days she suspected the boy didn't want to be loved.

He glared at the ground, nose scrunched and lips tightly pursed.

So much for nice. "Mister Saber, I asked you a question. I expect an answer. How often are you shifting?"

"Lots!" he wailed. The cub's bottom lip jutted out in a pout.

"Daily?"

"What's that mean?"

"Do you shift every day?"

A nod.

"More than once a day?"

Another nod.

Matron Rus sighed. "I expect you're hungry."

No response.

"Mister Rus, are you hungry?"

He shook his head. "I ate something."

"What?"

"I dunno. It hopped."

She blinked. "A rabbit? You ate one of the school rabbits?"

"Not a rabbit!" Justice said, sounding insulted. "It was black, and kinda crunchy. And small."

"A locust?"

"Do they look like giant grasshoppers?"

"Yes."

He nodded. "It tasted funny."

"You need more than a bug for dinner. Get dressed and I'll take you down to eat."

The cub nodded eagerly, a smile dimpling his cheeks.

She held out his blue duffel. "Your new bag."

The smile vanished.

"Justice," Matron Rus warned. "Every child at the crèche has their own bag. With name in it."

"It's no' my name," he muttered.

"Your name is Justice Saber Rus. You will write it in the bag, and then you may eat dinner."

He took the bag between thumb and forefinger—and dropped it on the floor.

Turning, the cub went to his locker and pulled out his clothes. He dressed slowly, with a furrowed brow of concentration. He turned to her, jaw set in a defiant line. "My name is not Justice Saber Rus."

"Yes, it is."

"That is your name for me," he said. "It's not my real name. My real name is what my family calls me."

Matron Rus closed her eyes. Would telling him the truth crush him? "Justice, the crèche is your family. We raised you. We named you. We're here for you."

"But you aren't my real family," the cub persisted.

"We're as real a family as you'll ever know."

Pale blue eyes narrowed. Justice growled.

"You are not here because I enjoy these arguments, Mister Saber. No one in the crèche is holding you hostage. We welcomed you in your infancy and gave you a home."

"Because no one else wants me," he whispered.

She sighed and sat on the footlocker, holding out a placating hand. "Not everyone can keep a child. There are times—"

"When it's okay to wrap a baby in a bag and put them in the trash?"

He'd been listening.

"No, Justice, there is never a time when that is acceptable."

Justice nodded. "I was stolen. A bad man took me from my real family, and threw me away. When my real family finds me I'll have a mommy and a daddy. And sisters. And cousins."

As fanciful delusions went it wasn't half bad. "No one stole you, Justice."

"Yes they did! My real family wants me! They have a real name for me!"

Matron Rus stood and pulled a pen from her pocket. "We're not arguing. You are here. This is your life. Until such a time as your family arrives to rescue you, your name is Justice Saber Rus. Write it in the bag, and you may eat."

"No." He crossed his arms.

She held the pen out, adamant. "Write. Or you will go hungry."

Justice stood in front of her, bag at his feet, and glared.

The sun set. Night crawled past.

Terssa Camlin Fisher snuck into the room to get someone's stuffed doll so the rest of the unit could sleep downstairs. Still the cub glared.

As dawn light filtered through the trees, fat tears rolled down the cub's cheeks. He grabbed the pen and sat.

Another hour passed with Justice staring at the bag.

"Write your name," Matron Rus ordered as the breakfast bell rang.

Shaking with rage, Justice opened the bag. She watched the tears fall as he scowled at the white tag. He sniffed. He opened the pen, leaned forward, and scribbled. Then, dropping it all, he stormed out of the room.

Matron Rus waited until she heard his feet running to breakfast before she bent down to inspect the bag. Only one word was inscribed on the tag:

NO

She folded the duffel and put it in Justice's footlocker. Forty years as a crèche matron had taught her patience— and that sometimes, a small bend could break a child. Justice could find his bag now. If he didn't shred it, then they were taking the first step toward healthy adulthood.

And, who knew? Maybe some day the boy named No would find his real family.

THE MAKING OF AN OVERLORD
Amy Laurens

HE SITS IN THE shuddering darkness with his arms clasped around the shoulders of his hound. The dog tolerates the confinement for just long enough to show he cares, then wriggles free and abuses his master's tear-stained face with kisses.

The boy laughs, then wraps one hand firmly over his own mouth, fingers sealing emotions in tight. His father must not hear. He pushes the hound, still only a handful of months old, away from his face and into the straw.

The dog is good-natured about the rejection, upending himself to present his belly and waving his paws invitingly. The boy obliges with a belly rub.

The magic comes questing, stinging like ice, smooth as seeping oil and just as false: a slick of shimmer overcoating magic that's meant to smother and claim and choke.

The boy's heart flutters like the pulse of a dying bird. He snatches at the dog. He doesn't let himself whisper 'no', because it's possible his father hasn't found him yet, is just checking in here to be thorough—but he isn't hopeful. Dread weighs him down like a bad meal, a meal he's been ingesting every day of his life through every pore in his skin. His body knows this feeling all too well, and leaps to familiar patterns: his mouth is dry, his fingers tremble, his throat's too tight to swallow. The tremouring staccato of his heart marks a rhythm his nerves are all too keen to follow; adrenalin and cortisol play two-part harmonies through his body.

It is the fear his father senses, like a predator drawn to prey, like an overlord drawn to weakness, like an abusive parent drawn to the only shape of their child that they recognise. The magic enfolds him, and his skin prickles.

Overlords will not waste their time on frivolous interactions, Father reminds him sternly in his head. *I've told your mother a thousand times the dog was a bad idea. But she coddles you.*

The magic winds tighter until it hurts to move. The hound pup quits straining against the boy's grasp and begins to whine.

The boy can just twitch his fingers to mimic rubbing the dog's ear, and the dog quiets.

You will be an Overlord, Deviran. It's what you were born to be, and you of all people should know that destinies must be fulfilled. Overlords cannot afford emotional attachment; it is unseemly. You want to do well, don't you? You want to make me proud? His father sounds confused, and Deviran hears the words he doesn't speak: How could I have fathered this son? Why is he never grateful for what I offer?

Tears that have no light to shine in fill Deviran's eyes. He blinks them back. "Yes, Daddy," he whispers through lips brittle as autumn leaves. *I want you to be proud.* He wants it so much that his chest hurts, and even if the magic wasn't drawing tighter still, he'd find it hard to breathe. "I want you to be proud."

The magic shifts, so subtlely that for a moment he doesn't understand what's changed. But then the dog yelps, convulses, and Deviran can't even move to draw him close, can't break the bonds of his father's restraint to show the only creature who's loved him in all the world that he's here, that he cares, that it hurts...

The dog convulses again, grunting and frothing interspersed with whines that shred against Deviran's chest. A paw shoots out in the darkness and claws rake against Deviran's face. He doesn't even feel the pain.

The tears that magic bids stay begin to fall regardless.

Now, says Father, *now you will be the Overlord that you are destined to become. Say thank you.*

Deviran cannot speak, cannot think, cannot move against the weight of the warm slip of happiness lying broken on his legs.

The magic grips him, arching him back until his spine protests with pain so hot it burns. *I said, say thank you!*

"Thank you!" Deviran gasps. "Thank you!"

The magic releases him and he falls on his back. He lies still for a moment, then, when he realises he can move again, twists sideways, curling his body around the pup who's still so warm and soft his dying doesn't seem real. The shuddering darkness closes in once more as the magic fades away, and Deviran mumbles oaths into the young dog's ruff.

I will avenge you.

I will never be my father.

I will never be an Overlord.

MIDSUMMER QUEEN
Liana Brooks

I NEVER UNDERSTOOD THE ones who said they feared the night. Light was the harbinger of evil in my world. The night gave me strength to live. Under the moonlight I had no bruises.

Midsummer was the worst. Long days shortened the hours of my freedom. I despised the spring blossoms, hated that the night was quickening away. Sometimes I prayed for an early winter. Deep frost, snow, hunger, starvation... none of those mattered if I could wrap myself in a blanket of darkness.

It is noon by the sundial and the garden is in full bloom. Summer solstice lanterns are hanging throughout the town and from the caverns of the kitchen I can hear the bickering of two old woman. Years of jealousy spill between them, a vile acid that's etched itself into the stone. From the balcony above, I hear the snide mocking of a second pair who feed on that acid hatred and give it life in their bosoms. Daylight makes a solemn mockery of all I love.

Quietly, I pull my sleeve down to hide handprints that blacken my flesh. Others think I wear the sleeves out of vanity, that I hide my moon-pale skin from the sun because I reject the summer's golden glow. It is not true. Had I no horror to hide, I too would embrace the sun. But how can I when it is nothing more to me than the witch's pyre?

"Iulia!" A maid calls my name and I am stolen from the gardens to the goblin's den. Beautiful as the first spring morning is the woman I have called Mother all my life. She is radiant and fair to behold. Praised by men, idolized by artists, all who see her bow in awe. They should tremble in fear, for that fair face hides a cruelty like no other. Not even a cat tormenting a mouse matches her for cold-hearted pain. I bow before her, fearing the lash of both her whip and her tongue.

"You are an ugly child." She has said so all my life.

"Forgive me. I know no other way to be."

Her gold slippers glitter in the sunlight as she stalks around me, a lioness looking for a weakness. "When I was your age there were men that avowed they would die if they could not dance with me. Kings went to war to win my hand. Maidens took their own lives because they saw me and knew they could never compare."

"M'lady is the greatest wonder of the modern world," I said. "Not even the sun is more radiant than she." This is the prayer I learned in childhood. My scripture is a paean of praise to the woman I hate most.

"Who would see my beauty slip away?"

"No one, my queen. The world would die for want of you."

"True." A leather crop caresses my cheek. It is her form of endearment. "Once I hoped you would reign beside me, the Little Queen. The moon to my sun. But it cannot be."

The cold leather digs into my cheek and I feel hot blood well up where the rough edge cuts me. "M'lady has other daughters, both radiant and fair." All are dead. The gravestones border the garden like a white marble fence. No beauty that competes with her is allowed to live. Yet she births daughters like a queen bee, always searching for her destruction. It makes her feel alive.

"Tonight we will have visitors to help us celebrate the solstice. Won't that be nice?"

Victims for the altar. Suitors from abroad. "They are lucky indeed that the most beautiful of all women allows them to walk in her presence." No matter what my heart feels, I must keep to the well-worn script.

The leather crop strikes across my back, a brief riff of pain between my shoulder blades. "Go. Make yourself presentable. Our guests will be on the altar before the sun sets."

So it is every year. Her sacrifice to the elder gods. Her assurance of power and beauty.

I flee the room and catch a glimpse of myself in the mirror. Pale skin, white as a winter moon, with hot red blood crusting on my cheek. My pale green dress is marked by the same blood on my back. My hair, crimson as my blood, is matted and filthy. Still, I lift my chin as I walk. The moon is rising, a pale assassin in the sky, and I can feel the strength it gives me.

No one marks my appearance. The servants never rush to help me. The queen only meets out punishment deserved. Why else would she beat her only living child?

In the cool darkness of my room near the dungeons, I bathe. The water sluices over me, washing away pain and fear. Resolution strengthens my sinews. Tonight, the moon rises early. Tonight, I too will ascend, either to flee this golden kingdom or to stand upon the altar as a sacrifice myself; I do not care. All I wish to do is escape the woman who gave me life. The woman who makes my every nightmare truth.

The bells ring in the square. The visitors are here. For them I shed no tears. Greed led them here, or lust perhaps. The wealthy widow queen whose beauty is beyond compare. They come to claim her, to take what is not theirs. In return she takes their lives to lengthen her own.

"Iulia." Her voice crawls through the darkness like a spider.

"Mother." I step out in my pale gray dress. My crimson hair is bound up under a dark gold veil. Tonight I am no more than a statue in my mother's menagerie.

Her cold fingers grasp my chin through the veil. "Do you not love me child? Have I not given you everything? Have I not laid aside my own desires to see you well? When you were ill, was it not I who sacrificed everything to win the favor of the elder gods and see you healed? Your father would have let you die, but what did I do?"

"You saved me."

"Yes, I saved you. I gave up everything I held precious so I could see you live."

How generous were the elder gods to give her endless life when all she asked for was a child's health... But this I do not say. I did once, and I learned how long it takes for bones to mend. "You are more generous than I can say," I whisper.

"Come, child. Walk with me. Our visitors must see how much I love my child."

The stone walls feel like a tomb, although I know my life will end in fire. One day my mother will tire of me. One day she will cease to toy with me and will slit my throat. Drink my blood. One day, she will offer me to the elder gods to capture another season in the sun.

Our footfalls lead to the garden, then down to the gate, and finally to the long white path to the square. The setting sun warms our backs. To the people waiting we are but two figures—one glowing and golden, one dark and severe—walking out of the light. They wait, hearts racing in their chests. The queen's magic stretches out, ensnaring them, entangling them in their own wanton wishes.

I look up at the high and pale moon. The sun is falling. The moon reigns.

Almost unbidden, the silver knife appears in my hand, hidden by the fall of my sleeve.

Beside me, my mother pauses. Sunlight dances along the knife edge and the whole world holds still. Which heart calls to this blade? Whose blood will drip from its curving silver tip?

"Iulia?" My mother looks so confused. "Whatever have I done to you, child, to make you hate me?"

The blade leaps for her throat and I whisper, "Everything."

WHAT BLOOD CAN DO
Amy Laurens

EIGHT YEARS AGO, MY father slaughtered my mother. He tied her down on the dining table with guy ropes and slit her throat with the bread knife. It wasn't sharp. There was so much blood I thought it would never stop.

I screamed. I thought I'd never stop.

My father left me there, ten years old and elbow deep in the pulsing river of my mother's life. He told me he was sorry. My fingers burned to use the knife on him. With blood tingling over my skin, I swore I'd have my revenge.

I called the cops, of course; I was ten, not stupid. I told them what I'd seen, and they bounced me along the foster-care chain after booking me appointments with Phyllis. She gave me lollipops and sympathetic glances over her gold-wired glasses. It didn't help. I had to see her, though, until at last I promised I was starting to heal.

I lied.

When I was fourteen, we did archery for sport at school. I loved it: it was soothing, focused—and practical. I sliced my finger on an arrow that first time, testing to see if it could kill a man. The blood got all over my bowstring. I never missed a shot.

I joined the local archery club, working clean-up in their café to pay the fees. I practiced every day, without fail. At sixteen, I was winning state tournaments. At seventeen, I won the nationals.

At eighteen, it was time to hunt him down.

On impulse, I sat down with a phone book. As I opened it, one page papercut my thumb and blood smeared across it. I hissed sharply, but dialled the bloodied number.

It was him; I'd know his voice beyond the grave.

He agreed to meet me at the Okahawa Trail, too eager for anything that smacked of reconciliation to have a sense of self-preservation. I shot him. It would have been a good, clean kill too, right in the throat—a nice sense of irony, I thought—but the arrow had been knocked a little off course by a freak gust of wind.

I could have walked away, left him to die. The bolt was only a standard cut-on-contact broadhead; any local deer hunter would have used the same. But since he was going to be alive for another minute, I figured he might as well know why I'd done it.

I didn't expect the tears. My own, I mean; I assume it's pretty normal for your eyes to fill with liquid when you've had your throat pierced and are about to die. But as I stood over him, desperately bricking up the wall around my feelings, tears welled up and overflowed. "You bastard," I whispered. "Why did you kill her?"

He stared up at me with eyes wide—fear, pain, guilt, who could tell?—gasping and gurgling as the blood oozed away.

My stomach knotted as I remembered: a bread knife, ropes tied to the dining table, my forearms tingling, up to my elbows in my mother's blood. Disgusted, I turned away.

"Wait," he rasped. "Stop."

I stopped, but didn't turn around.

"She... was trying... kill you."

I whirled on him. "How dare you. How *dare* you! You, you *murderer!*" I spat.

"Blood," he wheezed. "Her blood."

"Yes," I said, locking him in a steely glare. "There was a lot of blood. I should know; you abandoned me in it."

"Not... abandoned. Saved."

I snorted and stalked off.

"Cassie. Your blood. You never miss."

I froze. "How do you know that?" How could he possibly know the reason why the club members called me Zero? How did he know I'd never missed a shot?

"She... same. You get... from her."

I inched back around to face him, heart exploding in my chest. "What are you saying?"

"She... Your mother... Fae."

The rough trunk of a tree caught me as I lurched.

"The blood... you have her blood."

My mind whirled as I remembered every incident I'd passed off as coincidence, all those times I'd thought I'd just been lucky. Every time, the blood. "Why did you kill her?" I whispered.

"She would have killed you. The Blood"—I heard the capital letter this time—"calls to blood. Any... any daughter of hers... competition."

I sank to the ground beside my father. The ooze of red at his neck was coming thicker now. Desperation surged. I snatched at my sweater, tearing ineffectually before stripping it off to press against his wound. "She wanted to kill me?" I said, still whispering. This time, it wasn't the memories of luck that came, but of unluck: of all the times I'd nearly died before I was ten. The time I fell in the gap between the train and the platform; the time I fell from a second-storey balcony and rolled down concrete steps. My grandparents used to joke that I was made of rubber, that I was the most accident-prone child they'd ever seen.

I didn't have a single accident after I was ten.

"It wasn't... her fault," he said through the gasps. "The Blood. You have her power. It... drove her crazy. Blood... never share its power."

My father's blood seeped through my sweater and stickied my fingers. I stared at the red-streaked whorls of my left-hand fingerprints. Was it true? I snatched another arrow from my quiver and sliced the tip across my palm. I let the blood well for a moment. A tingling sensation covered the palm of my hand, familiar and comforting— and unright. It wasn't the feeling of injury, but something more; my lifeblood pulsing with energy—and power.

The truth crushed me, robbing my lungs of air. My mother had tried to kill me, more times than I could remember. My father had killed her to save me. And I'd come here for revenge.

I stared as the blood of the one who'd murdered to save me ebbed away. "I'm sorry," I whispered. "I'm so sorry."

He didn't answer, his face grey and clammy.

I hated him for killing my mother, even if she had been trying to kill me; I hated him for making me what I'd become, for not telling me, for not trusting me.

But I couldn't hate him if he was dead.

I pressed my wounded palm against his neck. My blood had been keeping me safe for eighteen years. Time to find out what it could really do.

WELCOME TO DARK DALE
Liana Brooks

THE SIGN WAS BROKEN. Fragments lay on the ground, splintered and splattered with blood. What remained of the rotting stomp in the ground was charred and gnawed on; teethed on, I corrected myself. There was still a tooth sticking out of the wood.

Marzrels went through several sets of teeth as babies—larvae? They were carnivorous worms and I'd never stopped to ask one what it called its young. Dinner maybe. But probably breakfast. Just another joy of Dark Dale.

A shadow caught my eye: a small, yellow scorpion no bigger than my thumb, darting away. I stepped on it. Those I occasionally called friends laughed at my odd footwear. They told me on numerous drunken occasions that I'd do better to leave the iron out of my boots and run faster. As I lifted my foot and used a second dagger to dig out the still-wriggling arachnid, I yet again disagreed with them. I killed the wriggler and left the body in the dust. One didn't survive the Dale by being kind and loving. Of course, I'd never asked anyone else about surviving the Dale; as far as I knew, I was the only one who could make the claim. Horrific death was about as native to the Dale as Marzrels.

I sauntered toward my destination, a nondescript rock of little intrinsic value, slashing at bushes and stabbing at shadows. The bushes burned and the sand crackled under the loving brush of my sword of fire. Most people liked to collect mementos of their adventures. The average sword-for-hire collected gold; others took bones, teeth, ears, treasure, whatever caught their fancy. A fair number in this region collected skulls.

I collected swords. The swords of slain heroes, and I'd killed every one. And because I knew the weapon I carried had already failed one protagonist, I also carried daggers.

At the rock, I paused and growled. This was the part of visiting the Dale that I didn't like. "I am she that is summoned. I am she that answers." I recited the chant from memory, paying minimal attention as the rock steamed and smoked. The smoke coalesced and formed into an ashen-skinned demon with glowing silver eyes.

"Took you long enough didn't it?" the creature demanded petulantly. "Do you know how long I've been waiting?"

"Two days," I guessed, since I had only received the summons two days ago—in the middle of a barroom brawl no less, which had been most inconvenient. "You were here last time. Make someone in the council mad, did we?"

The demon sniffed. "You know not of what you speak, mortal!"

"Of course I know of what I speak, and don't call me mortal unless you intend to prove the point." My free hand wandered closer to the abyssal whip I had picked off the body of a half-eaten necromancer.

Some people would never learn to leave well enough alone. At least not in this life.

"You will die!" the demon cried.

Demons did this sort of thing; it was habit more than anything else and not something that had particularly bothered me once I realized they all did it. I was nearly eight when that happened. Some little girls played with dolls, or horses, or looms, or swords, but I was deprived, forced to play with demons because I lacked parental supervision and income.

"You'll die too, eventually," I observed. "Does that make you mortal?"

"Of course not." The demon peered at me. "One of these days I'm going to make you flinch."

"Don't count on it," I advised.

It shrugged. "Here." It held out a miniature portrait and dropped it at my feet. "Kill this."

I picked up the likeness of a brawny man. "Nicely painted. Oils?"

"Oils?" the demon asked. "How should I know?"

"You didn't paint this?" I looked at him suspiciously. Having a demon hire me was not unheard of, but if this demon was hiring me for its own reasons, no other creature should have painted the likeness.

"It was given to me by the council." The demon looked as apologetic as it could.

"This is a council assignment?" The answer was important: it affected pay.

I always charged the council more. It was spite, and I'd be the first to admit it. I didn't like the council. One of the idiots on it sired me—possibly mothered me, I wasn't quite sure. But I was spawned by one of them and they'd dropped me in the mortal realm with no more than a spell book and a handful of silver. Hardly decent parenting, in my book. Gold was what loving parents gave to their spawn—or offspring, species-dependent.

The demon rubbed the bald space between its horns. "You won't charge too much, will you?"

"For a rush job on a brawny barbarian?" I tossed the miniature in the air and caught it thoughtfully. The demon's silver eyes followed the portrait. "Triple my usual rates for a rush job. Plus the weight of the hero in gold."

His eyes snapped to my face. "Outrageous! You worked for the liche in the summer valley for a quarter of that for the same sort of outlander!"

I tossed the portrait to the demon and shrugged. "Then find another assassin. If you can find one who will survive."

That was my trump card every time. No one survived Dark Dale. Those that didn't die outright were turned. Some were zombies, some liches, others hideous constructs of the Madness, souls ripped and torn beyond recognition. The lucky ones (or unlucky, depending on your moral outlook) were turned into lesser demons: imps, succubae, incubi, and other half-mad things that did the bidding of the powerful. They would never be true demons, not with parts of their human souls intact, but they lived like demons.

"Double plus the weight," the demon bargained.

"Triple plus the weight." I stood firm. "You won't be able to find anyone else." The demon grumbled something foul under its breath. "Just tell yourself it comes out of the council's treasury, not yours."

The demon tossed its head in a nod. "Not my soul," it muttered. "Find the hero. Kill the hero. And your pay will arrive as usual."

"Good enough," I agreed placidly. Most humans don't know that demons are actually bound by their words—unlike humans, who can lie constantly without punishment. No blood or vows are needed, just a firmly-worded agreement. The demon's promise was contingent on my finding and killing the hero, but since I *would* find and kill said hero, there was no problem. "How many days ahead is this hero?"

The demon held up three pointed talons. "He nears the east gate even now. Within two moonrises he will have reached the portal."

"Are you not attacking him?" I asked with more suspicion than usual.

"We have thrown everything at him since he arrived."

"The east gate is nearly impossible to reach unless you have a demon guide," I noted. "Does he have a demon guide?"

"No." The ashen demon squirmed.

"Tell me," I ordered.

"He is impervious to magic. He nulls it. Nothing we do works." The demon, with its monstrous horns, bulging muscles and venomed talons, pouted.

I sheathed my sword of fire and pulled out a sharp iron spike. "Is he mortal or a demigod?"

"Mortal, most assuredly."

I gave the demon a pointed look.

"Probably mortal," it amended with an apologetic shrug. "No divine influence has been seen on him."

"Well, that at least is encouraging." I traded my iron dagger for my favorite offhand weapon: a sword breaker.

There are two kinds of sword breakers readily available for those who want to crush their enemies and deprive them of hope. The first is the traditional iron rod with no sharp edge. It's heavy, sword-length, and if you strike hard enough, swords break. The second is a long dagger with a sharp edge on one side and a deep-set jagged edge on the other side. You catch your opponent's weapon in the deep-set serrations and twist. Snap! Such a lovely sound and so useful when you are forced into confrontation with berserkers, especially those who tie their souls to their blades. The look of panic as they realize their pride has killed them is priceless.

Well, no, not priceless; I can put a price on anything.

"Well," I told the demon. "I'd better get going then." I gave it a sardonic smile. "Tell the Council hi from me."

It glared at me. "Tell them yourself." Smoke puffed and the demon vanished.

I rolled my eyes at the theatrics and hefted my sword. Time to give our barbarian friend a nice old Dark Dale welcome—the traditional way.

WREATH-BEARER
Amy Laurens

ADRENALIN FRISSONED FROM STOMACH to fingertips as I landed on a cold, cobbled floor, the foot-thick door slamming shut behind me, blocking out the festival sounds as suddenly as if I'd died. I hadn't, though; my panting gasped echoed in the absolute darkness of the Tower—until I stopped to wet dry lips and realised someone else was breathing too.

My heart leapt. I scrabbled backwards against the door; the long, rattling breaths drew closer.

Something touched my foot. I screamed, flinging myself at the spelled wood that separated me from life. Long splinters tore off in my fingertips and blood soaked my nail beds—and something touched my shoulder.

I froze. I screwed my eyes closed, little panicked breaths my only movement.

"Greetings, Wreath-Bearer."

The whispered voice scraped over me like bones rattling in the wind, and I huddled my face against the door. "Please," I whispered, chest heaving. "Don't hurt me."

Cold fingers trailed down my spine. "We will not hurt you, so long as you bear the wreath."

My fingers convulsed against the splintered door. The wreath. I'd dropped the wreath. I whirled around, slamming my back against the wood. Where had I dropped it? It could be anywhere in the dark, it could be—

Against all odds, the wreath lay at my feet, and I could see it: orange flowers bound into a circle with bright orange ribbons, glowing faintly in the midnight dark. I glanced to where I'd last heard the voice, then snatched the wreath from the ground and hugged it to my chest. "I've got it," I said, voice barely tremouring. "You can't hurt me now. You said."

Voice susurrused around me, buffeting me from all sides. "Cannot hurt you... Will not harm... The wreath... The wreath! ... Lead us on..."

I clutched the wreath tighter. "Who... Who are you?"

The whispers rose again, but before I could make out words the first voice spoke. "You know who we are, and what we require. We are the dead. You will lead, and we will follow."

Licking my lips again, I nodded. "Yes. Lead you." My shoulder blades dug against the door and my chest still heaved. I scrunched my eyes closed against the eternal darkness. Lead the dead. Why me? Why *now*? A sob strangled me as I thought of the sky blue dress tucked away in a closet at my mother's house, a dress I'd never need wear now. One day. Just one more day, and I'd have been safely married.

I swiped furiously at the tears that breached my eyelids. "Yes," I said, more strongly this time. "Yes, I am here to lead you."

I was here to lead them, and lead them I would, because I was part of the Tower now, and no one ever came out of the Tower. If I couldn't lead them to the top, I'd die and become one of them, a restless spirit doomed forever to haunt the Tower until someone came who *could* lead us.

"What... What happens if I lose the wreath?" I asked, eyes still closed.

Soft breezes swept my cheek, my forehead, my hair. "Feya," the voices whispered my name. "Feya."

My heart hammered in my chest. *"What will happen to me?"*

The first voice, the loudest, replied. "If the wreath is lost, we will make you one of us. Then you will hope that the next Wreath-Bearer succeeds where you will have failed."

I swallowed. It had been nineteen years since the last successful Wreath-Bearer. Chances were not great that I would succeed where many stronger had failed. I clenched my jaw and hugged the wreath to me, burying my face in the uppermost flowers. They smelled like sap and honey and death. "How will I know the way?" I murmured, mostly to myself.

But this time, the breath against my cheek was almost warm. "Feya." I could hear the smile in the speaker's voice, but I still clutched the wreath over my heart like a shield. "Open your eyes."

The air hitched in my throat, suddenly too dry to pass with ease. Open my eyes? Visions of dry, desiccated corpses filled my mind's eye, corpses that shambled and hobbled while strips of decaying flesh hung from their bones, and suddenly opening my eyes was less horrifying than keeping them closed. I looked, and gasped.

Silvered figures danced and swirled in front of me, long hair flying, mouths open wide in silent, delightful laughter. The moment they realised I could see them, they turned, crowding in on me, hands outstretched in welcome.

"Come," they whispered. "Come dance with us. Lead us in the dance." They whirled off and away, smiling, laughing, eyes bright and shining, and as they divided I saw between them a path, gilded and silver, insubstantial as moonlight, real and solid as hope.

My heart still hammered, but what other choice did I have? With my shoulders I pushed away from the door that had been gouged by fearful hands innumerable and stepped onto the shining path. The wreath exploded into light in my hands, warm and crimson like a phoenix. It swirled around me, then moved forward. I followed, and the ghosts of decades past came too.

RED PLANET REFUGEES
Liana Brooks

BLUE LIGHTNING ARCHED THROUGH red clouds boiling on the horizon. The sun hung low, a reminder of the day to come, a reminder of searing heat and the outpost's dwindling water supply. I pulled another shirt off of the line and risked a peek at the dark horizon.

Nothing.

The distant galaxies were too faint to be seen, and there were no near stars. We were the last outposts, the last human refuge before nothingness. But I didn't care about that; I was looking for the ice ship. Every year it was a race. The original colonists were left with a single vessel to conduct basic observations and experiments. When the domes failed, that single ship moved my ancestors to the outpost monitoring the storm world. And now that one ship collected ice from the rings farther out to give us the water we needed to survive.

I didn't expect them today, or tomorrow, or even soon. We still had six months' worth of water left, if nothing went wrong. We could survive that. But I still looked.

Taking the last shirt off the line, I waved to my neighbor. The gray-haired matron was the eldest of her small clan and the only one I knew on sight. The rest she kept cloistered inside their dome, safe from the radiation of the sun. I didn't have anyone protecting me. I didn't have anyone to protect. My only brother left after his wife and son died. My parents died years before that in a rationing scare; we'd survived while they wasted away from dehydration.

Instinctively, I checked the water levels as I walked inside. All the monitors showed the tank three-quarters full. Good enough for now. I turned on the radio as I dumped clean linens on my make-shift bed and debated hanging my last few wet things on the line.

"Good morning everyone! This is Joe and Jo! Twenty-three minutes to full sunrise and it's already one hundred and ten outside. Looks like it'll be a hot one!" Joe yelled through the radio.

His wife, Jo, came on with a higher-pitched but equally-enthusiastic tone. "Hiya folks! Are you all ready for the day? Is your laundry in? Your dishes washed? Great! Because we have a full load of fun for you!"

I tossed my last suits into my basket and walked back outside. They were mostly dry and if I pulled them in within an hour, nothing would burn.

Coming back, I sealed the door behind me as the Hilda's Children's Chorus sang the wake-up song. The radio chimed and the family in charge of monitoring water gave their daily report. Everything was fine, water levels were great, consumption was slightly up in the greenhouse because of the new seedlings being at 'that stage', but things were expected to level out in about seventeen days.

The radio chimed again and Jo cut in. "That was great kids! I'm glad to hear you so perky on this hot, hot day!"

"And thank you to the Dugroot clan for watching our water supplies. It's a grave responsibility and for the last eight generations the Dugroots have proven they're willing to sacrifice to see the rising generation watered," Joe said, giving the word 'grave' extra emphasis.

"Now that we've had the good news, let's try some bad news!" Jo enthused.

"Over to you, Jessa!" Joe said.

The radio chimed as I slid into my usual seat and pulled my microphone close. I smiled just like my brother taught me and started talking. "It's a wonderful morning over here at Far Out Skywatch and let me tell you, folks, there is nothing to see. Not a blessed blip on the radar screen. We are well and truly alone. But that's the bad news; let's try some more good news!"

"You have good news?" Jo cut in from the radio's main control panel.

"Believe it or not, Jo, I do!" I said, matching her enthusiasm. "Last dark we got a call from the ice ship. They're doing well and they sent their letters home." I pulled out my notepad and started reading. "Johnny sends May his love and says he hopes to be home in time for the baby. Trounce says 'hiya' to Ma and his brother. Matthew wants to let his clan know he's learning piloting and catching now, and making them proud. And young Egglebert, who's on his first tour, sends to say 'hiya' to all the folks at home, the view is great, and he's loving everything, and then the captain cut him off." I paused, imaging the clans gathered around the radio for our communal morning show laughing.

"The good Captain Tryer says to tell y'all that the ship's fuel is at eighty-seven percent and they're catching extra ice with the new nets that we rigged last season. Everything is in good working order; food supplies and morale are high.

They expect to spend another twelve weeks catching and hope to bring home extra water this season.

"That's all I got, folks. This is Far Out Skywatch, if something happens I'll let you know!"

Jo and Joe took over as I switched off my radio. As I folded clothes and bathed, Jo and Joe prattled on, telling jokes, discussing books, and asking questions of the various clans.

As they started the 'Too Hot to Talk' song, I pulled on my shoes to get the last of the laundry off the line. I laughed at the stale jokes. There were only seventeen families that had survived the past two-hundred-plus years of hardships; eventually we'd run out of things to say. But Jo and Joe kept morale high while we waited each season for crops to grow in our dimly-lit gardens and the ship to return with ice, all the while praying to some deity none of us knew that one day the nations that had sent our forefathers out would come back to rescue us.

I paused by the sealed door and touched the little calendar that my father had left. Eighty-eight. Eighty-eight seasons until inbreeding, faulty technology, or lack of food killed us. The first refugees to arrive at the outpost had calculated how long they thought we could survive and made the calendar. By now most people had thrown theirs away in despair, but I kept ours, carefully removing one number each season, wondering if my ancestors who had carved the 324 pieces of wood ever imagined that we would still be on this planet when the wood ran out.

The radio chimed. I looked over my shoulder, frowning. I really needed to get my laundry in before the temperatures soared, but it was rude to keep someone waiting. The radio chimed again. With a shrug I walked over to the radio station, my finger tracing down the line of lights to see who was trying to contact me.

Red four. Who was red four?

I hit the red light and my radar screen lit up green and black. I blinked as the radar blipped.

A blip?

What did that mean? My brother had taught me maintenance but he never mentioned blips.

I hustled to the back room where we kept the ancestors' books, diaries, and valuables tucked away for a future generation of refugees. I dragged my finger across the titles, trying to read fast enough to find the book I wanted in a hurry. There, written in Geek, a technician's manual for the radar array.

I pulled it down and scanned for a picture that matched my blipping radar. I found it a quarter of the way through the book. The caption read, 'Long Distance Array Radar Reading An Incoming Vessel.'

My heart stuttered as I skimmed the chapter. The black and green radar was the long-distance, deep-space radar, entirely different from the familiar red land-tracker that followed the ice ship landing.

I ran back to my radio and slammed my palm on the call button. "Hiya, folks, this is Far Out Skywatch and, um, according to the technician's manual I'm reading, the deep-space array has been activated by a, a..." I sucked in a long breath and spat out, "by an incoming hyperspace vessel that isn't broadcasting the pre-programmed security clearance.

"Folks." I grinned wildly. "We have visitors."

⌁⌁⌁

THE PECULIAR CLAUSTROPHOBIA OF LONELINESS

Amy Laurens

WE SAT APART, WATCHING the Earthrise. I wondered how many people were left down there.

"It's too crowded," she said abruptly. "I can't think in here."

I looked around our transparent dome, edge to edge a hundred paces, only us inside. "Where will you go?" We'd had this conversation before. We both knew there was nowhere.

"Get rid of the weeds," she told me instead. "The grass can't breathe."

This was new. "What should I do with them?"

"Burn them," she snarled, then slumped. "Or don't. Save the oxygen. I don't care. The rescue ship will come."

"It will." I hugged her, and waited for the mood to pass.

⌁⌁⌁

Later, I caught her staring at the stars. I anchored her hand in mine. "Whatcha thinking?" My pulse hammered.

She gestured over our heads, entranced. "Do you think they have enough room?"

"Who?" I asked, biting my lip as she pulled away.

"The stars."

They glittered the sky, crammed in elbow to elbow until some overlapped. I shrugged. "How much is enough?" A whole world wasn't enough when you shared it with EBOV *momento mortis*. And a dome was plenty if you didn't. I found Earth close to our western horizon and stared.

She squeezed my hand. "The rescue ship will come."

I nodded, still staring at Earth. "Of course." What if her mood didn't pass this time?

"It's the horizon," she said that night. "It's too empty. It's claustrophobic."

I shook my head and rested my head on her shoulder. "How can empty space be claustrophobic?"

She sighed and patted my hair. "Go to sleep."

In the morning, the airlock alarm screamed. I ran to it, sweat slicking my palms, fear clogging my throat, reaching for the emergency lock. But I was too late.

She'd left a note. It read: *I'm sorry. I needed space.*

I looked around the dome that I now inhabited alone. So much space, pressing down. She was right. It was too much emptiness to bear alone; it was smothering, cloying. Claustrophobic. I opened the airlock and hoped someone from Earth would survive.

No. Not some*one*. Some*ones*. Earth was far too large for one person to inhabit alone.

PERFECT DESTRUCTION
Amy Laurens

THE WIND HOWLS THROUGH the forest trees as Kiana stomps her combat boots to warm her feet. "Reckon they'll be much longer?" she says, adjusting her rifle in the crook of her arm.

Beside her, Heiman shrugs, carbon-fibre body armour blunting his movements. "Hope not. This wind's a killer."

Kiana casts a glance at the fence behind her: cast iron, eight feet high, practically indestructible. But clouds are gathering, pressure is building, and their shift ended ten minutes ago. "I'm going to climb the tree."

"Why d'you wanna do that for?"

A sharp crack. They both whirl around. A branch lies on the ground, broken by the fierce wind.

"Place is giving me the creeps," Kiana says, neck prickling. It feels like ants are crawling over her waist and hips. She shifts, wriggles, but her body armour's doing its job well and she can't get the itches to quit.

Big, grey cumulo-nimbuses boil over the sun.

"Doesn't matter," she says. "Home tomorrow."

"Oh?" says Heiman. "Tour's over?" His voice is too light, too casual.

Kiana doesn't look at him. "I thought you knew. This is my last shift."

He shrugs, picking at his rifle's grip where the parts don't quite line up.

Rumbling sounds in the distance. Heli rotors, or just thunder? Kiana hops from one foot to the other. "Wish they'd bloody hurry up."

"I dunno," Heiman says, staring fixedly at the treetops. "I'm in no rush."

Kiana eyes him sideways. He knew today was her last day. Everyone knew. The shifts are posted on the public roster board; it's not like it was a secret.

The rumble dies away. Just thunder then. The storms roar like the devil here, but they're transient, gone in under an hour.

"I'm climbing the tree."

Heiman shrugs. "Suit yourself."

Kiana straps her rifle on her back, adjusts her boots, and heads over to the lookout tree. She climbs the ladder to the platform that sways high above the fence and looks out over the forest. To the north the trees diminish and in the distance bare hilltops poke through, grass long and yellow. To her left the sun should be slowly toiling towards the horizon, but the storm clouds bubble and bloom like ink in the clear blue sky. No sign of helicopters in any direction and it's now—she checks—nearly twenty minutes past shift change. They've never been this late before.

She's going home tomorrow.

Cheek in her teeth, Kiana swings slowly southward. The iron fence stretches out below her, as far as she can see through the trees. It encloses a space hundreds of acres across, and she's never seen one of their charges in the flesh, but looking in there still gives her the creeps. The trees are taller, straighter, shinier, everything lush and green and perfect. Blossoms bear perfectly shaped petals, bloom into unblemished fruits, drop picture-perfect seeds.

She blinks. Was that a flash of white amongst the trees? Adrenalin floods her body and her stomach feels like it's dropped back to earth. She peers closely, but everything looks normal. With a forceful exhale, Kiana turns and crosses the platform to the ladder.

Another hum. Her head snaps around towards it, and there in the east like a giant black wasp: a helicopter powering towards her. Tension melts away and Kiana laughs. "Heiman!" she shouts. "Heiman, they're here!" She waves to catch his attention, laughing and pointing at the helicopter. Home. They're here, and she's going home.

The humming rumble grows louder as Kiana climbs down the ladder. Midway down, she realises the noise has changed in tone. It's not just the helicopter anymore—but it doesn't sound like thunder, either.

"What is it?" Hayman calls to her.

She looks around, but the trees are blocking her view. Hurriedly she scrambles to the top of the ladder again. Adrenalin floods through her: a unicorn, blinding white against the bright green grass, heading towards the fence. "Look out!" she screams. "Heiman, get away!"

He peers up at her, confusion knotting his brow, then turns slowly towards the enclosure.

The unicorn picks its way closer, like it has all the time in the world, and with every step the humming increases.

Kiana sees the moment Heiman spots the 'corn: his whole body stiffens, fingers tightening compulsively around his rifle. "Shoot! Shoot it! Shoot it now!" she calls.

The unicorn covers another ten metres before Heiman collects himself enough to raise the herb-loaded rifle.

The unicorn stops and throws its head back, point arcing up towards the gathering storm. Kiana runs her gaze across the sky and her heart skips another beat; the storm isn't coming, it's here.

And then in the same instant, three things happen. A shaft of crackling energy shoots up from the unicorn's point to the clouds; lightning strikes Kiana's tree; Heiman remembers his rifle and pulls the trigger.

Kiana screams as the tree trunk snaps, a sound like a canon firing, all death and inevitable destruction. She catches a quick glimpse of Heiman's face, staring up at her, mouth and eyes wide in horror. She's grabbing blindly, wildly, for anything she can reach. As she clings to one of the platform's rails the tree falls, and she rides it all the way into the cast-iron fence.

The fence should stop her, catch the tree—but either the storm or the unicorns have done something to it and instead the impact of the tree snaps it like brittle candy. It shatters on the ground, followed by the tree—and Kiana.

Hurts.

She sucks air in, shallow gasps that don't help to restore the breath that's been knocked out of her. A voice fades in, like her ears had stopped working during the fall or the crashing of the tree and fence and sky blocked everything out or maybe even like the world had ended.

"Get away! Get away from her, you pissing beast!"

Kiana can't move her head yet; her entire view is sky, framed on one side by branches.

Heiman rushes into her field of vision, standing protectively over her while she gasps like a fish out of water. Hurriedly he empties the clip from his rifle and tries to load another—but his fingers are fumbling and he drops it in the grass.

White. The sky shouldn't be white.

Fur. The sky is neither white nor furry.

Kiana's eyes widen as she realises the unicorn is close enough to touch, if only she could remember how to make her arms and fingers work.

Before she can think too hard about why her arms and legs aren't working, why she should be in so much pain after a fall like that and instead can't feel a thing, before she can verbalise the niggling terror lurking in the depths of her mind that something is wrong, Wrong, WRONG, light explodes from the unicorn. It's white and blinding in a way that no natural light could ever be: even the moon has warmth compared to this.

Her toes and fingers tingle. She can feel them. Her lungs burn, her hip—her hip is probably on fire.

Above her, Heiman groans, stumbles, falls to one knee.

"No," Kiana whispers as the burning in her lungs dies down. "No, you can't." But the unicorn's power is destroying him as fast as it's healing her, and when she leaps to her feet she's only just in time to catch him as he sways. He's too heavy for her to hold; she eases him slowly to the ground. "No," she tells him. "You passed medical. You passed!"

He smiles—tries to. It clearly hurts and his eyes unfocus through the pain. "F... Faked genes," he breathes raggedly.

Kiana presses her eyes closed tightly against his confession. "You idiot."

"Never... mind," he gasps out, eyes pressed closed. "You're going... home tomorrow."

"Too right," Kiana says. "I'm not sitting by *your* bedside for a month while they genewash you."

He laughs, weakly. "Get out," he says and gestures to the sky with his eyes.

Kiana glances over her shoulder: the heli is landing. By the time she looks back, Heiman is *gone*. She grips him for a second longer, fingers knotting in the loose sleeves of his uniform. Then she gently lays him down and stands. With deliberate, precise steps, she walks to the unicorn. She stares it in the eye, and languidly it stares back.

"You killed him. You *bastard*," she spits, hands fisting at her sides. "You *killed* him."

The unicorn just stands there.

Kiana throws herself at the immovable beast. She hammers her fists against its neck, kicks its fetlocks and screams. Someone races in behind her, pins her arms against her sides. She screams again, wordless rage, clawing and biting at whoever holds her.

The air is dark green and savoury, frabah rounds exploding, pop-pop-pop-pop-pop.

The unicorn shrieks. Kiana's head rings.

A white, glowing body rears, shrieks again, then stumbles to the ground.

The hands clamping Kiana's arms release her, and she falls. It hurts her knees. She doesn't care. She presses her hands over her face and cries.

The unicorn is dead—but so is Heiman.

THE DOG IS DEAD
Liana Brooks

A PALE HALF-MOON HUNG above the pine trees as I walked in the noon sun, wishing instead that I could run. It mocked me with the promise of a life I couldn't have, shouldn't want. The wind whispered, stirring the flowers around my feet as they wilted. I was no good at gardening.

I wasn't good at much, actually. But it was no big deal. Maybe a few hundred years ago when humans had eked out a living by growing their own food it would have mattered, but in the modern world where schooling was a matter of tissue programming and roles were chosen for everyone by a government program decades before they were born, being useful wasn't necessary.

The entire purpose of *my* life was to exist. My parents had money, which was nice. It meant they could afford to own land here on Earth and buy me a modest education when I turned ten: three hours of reading, writing, and basic mathematics programming straight into my cerebrum. When I was fifteen, my parents bought me a secondary education, allowing me to discuss classic literature with everyone else in my social strata. We'd all been program-med with the same six lectures, so our conversations usually devolved into recitations, seeing who could remember them best.

At eighteen I was tested, found intelligent enough to receive a basic civilian file (programmed into my head in fifteen minutes), and shunted into Slot 37B-12D5: housewife. If my parents had been poor, we would have been relocated to Prima, the main lunar base that hung like a golden star over the moon's surface. If they'd been wealthier, I would have received a fuller education that prepared me for more than balancing a check-book. If I'd been more intelligent, I would have earned a place among the scientists who filled Stellar base on the far side of the moon, the ones who'd be first chosen for any new colonies in the stars beyond.

In the secret watches of the night, when I stepped away from my cold bed to gaze at the stars, that's what I wished for. Something new. A glimmer of opportunity to be someone else. To remove the choking grip of societal norms and replace it with the heady sensation of not knowing what would happen next.

But here, in the noon light, under a half moon white as the clouds, I knew I would never have those things. I knew it as a child, and I would remain faithful to that truth until the day I turned ninety-seven and reported to the hospital to be humanely put down, sure in the knowledge that some young girl would arrive at my house the next morning to wear my clothes and walk my dog, because that is what Citizen 37B-12D5 does three times a day, rain or shine.

Of course, it wasn't a real dog, which would be cruel. It was a Canine Companion with FeelReal-Furr and a life-like bark. None of my schooling included information on dogs, so I had no words to describe it... Him... Her...

It. That bothered me. I wished I knew what words to say if I ever brought my pet up in conversation, but I didn't. I never would.

It was black. It came to my knee. It was programmed to need five kilometers of walking every day, which ensured I received the necessary exercise for my age and metabolism. With one last wistful glance at the moon I checked the mail (nothing) and returned to the house.

As I did every day, I watered a bowl of dead petunias on the front step, swept the wooden floors, and checked that the computer had ordered dinner for us. We were having pot roast. Everyone on the block was having pot roast. As far as I knew, everyone in my social strata was eating pot roast tonight. With slightly overcooked carrots and a choice of water or apple juice to drink.

I didn't want pot roast. I didn't want to water petunias. I didn't want to wait for another hour until my lawfully wedded husband arrived home from his government job to eat dinner. I went to the door, twisting the handle, even though I knew it was futile.

A melodic chime signaled the end of my momentary rebellion. "This door is locked for your security. Please state the reason you wish this door opened at this time."

"I want to go outside." My hand dropped to my side. I knew it was fruitless. It wasn't in the script. Citizen B37-12D5 never went outside in the afternoon.

"Did you forget to check the mail?" the computer asked.

"No."

"Would you like to watch some television?" Unbidden the television in the corner turned on, showing a comedy about life in the corporate world. "Your friends and neighbours all enjoy this show. Why not join them in a light-hearted laugh as Randi and Co. try to make Mister Meeker forget his glasses?"

"I don't wish to watch television. I want to go outside."

"Perhaps you would like to call a friend?" the computer suggested.

"I would like to go outside."

"Why don't you log in to your social network and plan a picnic? Everyone loves picnics." A screen on the kitchen table shimmered to life and showed a running stream of the thoughts of my 'friends'. They were all very similar; we did all have the same twenty-thousand-word vocabulary after all.

"Thank you," I lied to the computer. "That sounds very engaging."

I sat down and watched as people typed the lines from the show as it played behind me in the living room. As Mister Meeker outsmarted Randi and Co. once again, a gray car drove up to our house. My husband exited it, checked his tie, locked the door, and counted forty-eight steps precisely.

The door unlocked for him and he stepped inside. "Hello, dear. You look well. Did you have a good walk with the dog?"

"Yes." The word was past my lips before I even considered another option. "Dinner is ready."

"Good. I had a busy day. I'm hungry."

I mouthed the words with him. In four years living together, our conversation never varied. Sometimes I wondered if he was as robotic as the canine companion now lying inactive by the fake fireplace. "What would you like to drink?"

"Water, please."

I stood, and again rebellion flared. I arranged our dinner plates and gave us both apple juice. Instead of taking the eight carrots allotted to me I piled all sixteen carrots on his plate and took both slices of meat. "Dinner is ready."

My husband took off his tie and looked at our plates. "D... d... d..."

"Your line is, 'Dinner looks delicious.'" I folded my napkin on my lap and waited for him to sit.

After a moment he sat beside me. "Dinner looks different."

"I tried something new today. You'll like it." I hoped I was lying. I hoped he hated it. I hoped he threw his plate and broke a window so I could run out through the glass and watch the moon set in the darkness.

He ate his carrots. "Dinner was delicious. Thank you."

And it was over.

Now he would go to shower, change into a bathrobe, and watch two hours and thirty-one minutes of television before yawning once and going to bed.

I sat at the table staring at the two slices of meat on my plate.

I was only hurting myself by not eating. No one else would notice. No one else would care. And if by some small chance I was able to resist food for days on end until I made myself sick, I would only be transferred to the hospital and be reprogrammed. Or put down.

I dumped the meat on the canine companion's food bowl, on top of the fake kibble I put in for verisimilitude. The canine companion could only eat on command and I'd never ordered it to eat before. Now I did. "Dog. Eat."

Wagging its tail, the robotic construct chewed on the real meat—and choked. Its eyes sizzled for a moment, flashing red, and then it fell over with a hollow clang.

My husband laughed at something on the television.

I walked over, standing in front of the screen so I could block his view. "The dog is dead."

My husband struggled. This wasn't part of the script. This is not what we did every day. This was new.

I nearly clapped with joy. This was new! I didn't know his answer! I didn't know what came next!

"Why is the dog dead?"

"The dog ate food. The dog choked. The dog is dead."

My husband stood up and turned to look at the canine companion. "Dogs should not eat people food." He sat back down and laughed even though the television was showing a commercial for toothpaste. Everyone loved that commercial. When I ordered groceries online on Tuesdays, the screen always told me it was the one my friends liked.

I wondered about that. Was there any other kind of toothpaste? If I wanted to buy something that none of my friends had tried, would the computer let me? Would I like it if I did?

There was no way of knowing. I sat beside the dead dog. My husband watched his television shows and went to bed. The lights in the house turned off. The steady hum of electronics died as the computer decided we were asleep.

Why it followed his schedule and not mine, I wasn't sure. The computer would remind my husband to go to bed, but never me. Once he was home and I was safely locked inside, nothing else seemed to matter. Proof that the computer was just as dumb as everyone else.

I watched the moon set, Prima shining like a gem.

Was there someone out there who wanted to be me? Did that person have a number like I did, a place in society like mine? Or did they have a name?

I showered after the moon set, got dressed, and lay in bed waiting for sleep to come. It never did. I wasn't tired. I was bored. I wanted... something. I wanted to go outside.

When my husband woke up early, I picked up the dog and followed him to the door. This wasn't in the script. Fear filled his eyes.

"I'm putting the dog outside."

"I think the dog wants a walk." When in doubt, stick to the script.

We both looked at the spot where the canine companion should have been jumping with its tongue hanging out.

"Yes. I guess I should walk the dog."

He nodded. "Have a good day."

As the door closed, I shoved the dog's body in the way. The lock clicked shut and the television turned on the morning news.

I stepped outside as the reporter detailed what a beautiful morning drive it was today.

Canine companions couldn't walk on grass, so we always followed the sidewalk on a loop through the neighborhood, screened by pine trees. On the way I'd see glimpses of the highway in the distance. At one point you could even see the spires of the city buildings. I didn't know which city; geography cost extra.

This morning I walked on the grass, watching it bend under my heavy tread. Each step smothered to death countless plant cells. I was incautious. Uncaring. I reveled in their tragic demise.

I twisted the toe of my shoe into the turf, relishing the feel of grass dying under foot. I imagined little screams of plant terror echoing to the cold stars above. I imagined the gasp of shock and denial as someone from Prima looked down and saw me savagely destroying a plant they could never touch because they were banished from the very planet of their birth.

The sweet scent of cut grass invigorated me. I ran.

Over the lawns and past the pines I ran, to the edge of the highway where auto-piloted cars flew past, their passage whipping my hair up. My heart raced as I realized I could end it all here. None of those cars could stop. None of the drivers even knew how to. I could leap and after a moment of blinding pain, everything would be over.

I jumped.

The cars stopped. They hung in the air like frozen hummingbirds, unreal.

Tentatively, I reached out a hand to touch a bright red cruiser. The car was hot. The driver inside looked back at me, confused, uncertain. We were off script. Off the script. Off the page. Off the writing desk and floundering.

I stepped through the space between cars. Skipping, dancing. They moved around, resumed their flow. Everything was as it should be except that here and there—wherever I stepped—they froze. I was the queen of chaos, suspending the birds in their flight.

Life happened around me as I wandered down the lines of the highway. People went to work. One car I stopped had an old man with a dark face, somber and sad. I knew without a word that he was on his way to the hospital to die. I stepped away and his car moved on, rolling with the tide of humanity to its destination, inevitable, unavoidable. Inescapable.

I followed. It was that or find my way back to the pine trees and the quiet suburban house where my canine companion lay dead. If I went back, the doors would lock. If the doors locked I'd never escape again. If I never ran, I'd never know how far I could go.

DREAM AWAY
Liana Brooks

"SIR, HOW WOULD YOU like to take your dream vacation today?" The young woman smiling at Jazin as he tried to hurry down the packed commuter tunnel was a perky little thing. Cute button nose, cinnamon-colored hair, and pale-gold freckles on skin a few shades darker than her hair. She waved a synthpaper brochure at him. "Where do you want to go?"

"Home," Jazin said, avoiding eye contact. "My bank account doesn't match my dreams."

She stepped out from behind the table, her ivy-green skirt swirling as she moved. "I have dream vacations for all budgets."

"Yeah?" And he was going to get a promotion to a corner office. Just as soon as the moon turned blue. "Does this dream vacation come with paid leave?"

The young woman smiled impishly. "No leave time required. This really is a *dream* vacation." With a touch of her finger the brochure projected a hologram of him on a white sand beach. "Do you know the average dream lasts less than five minutes? With Dream Away's new REMtech Dream 6K, you can have a week's worth of luxury in five minutes."

Jazin pushed the brochure away. "Thanks, but no thanks. I can't afford a vacation, real or otherwise."

"Oh, but you can!" she insisted. "Give me a minute, I'll give you the perfect day. Give me five minutes, and I'll give you a week in paradise. Give me an hour, and I can give you a lifetime!"

He shot her a skeptical glare. "You'll give me a sticky chair to nap in that stinks of other people and hasn't been sanitized in a week. Thanks, but pass." He sidestepped and kept walking.

"Come on," she cajoled, dancing to keep up. "What would it hurt to try it?"

"Yes. I'd like to pay my rent this week, thanks all the same."

She licked her lips and glanced back at the stall. "What if I... gave you a taste? For free."

He stopped outright and looked her over. "Sounds like you're pedaling hard addictives, lady."

"Oh, no!" She shook her head and her beaded earrings jingled a soft melody. "Dream Away's product is one hundred percent non-addictive."

Jazin rolled his eyes. "I bet. I nap, I walk away and the dream's forgotten in ten minutes anyway. Everyone knows dreams don't last."

"Dream Away dreams do." She placed a small, elegant hand on the crook of his arm and peered up at him, green eyes wide. "In one minute I can give you the perfect day. You want the corner office? It's yours. Want to be the star of your favorite sports team? Done. You want a day to catch up on your reading? I have all the books waiting for you. You'll feel the pages in your hands, smell the paper and ink, and when you open your eyes you'll remember the book just as if you'd spent the day reading."

He frowned. "And then I'll want another hit which will cost me—what—a day's wages? A week's? It's not worth it."

She shook her head determinedly. "Dream Away provides no more endorphins than you would get from a thirty minute run at the gym. And while we can't burn calories for you like a run will, we can offer you a reduction of mental stress. You won't get a real sunburn at the pool in the Jawamai Mountains. You won't really eat draris fruit in the orchards of the Old King. The new friends you meet won't be real. But you'll remember all of it like it was. It really is the perfect vacation."

"How will I remember it?" he demanded, gripping his briefcase tighter. "Are you going to dribble fruit juice on my chin?"

"Even things you experience while awake are merely secondary sensations processed by the brain. Originally created to combat depression, the REMtech Dream 6K is the delightful side outcome of Dr Wria's research into retraining brains after traumatic injury. While it initially relied on pre-programmed dreamscapes, Dream Away is now sensitive enough to respond to sensations perceived by your brain, allowing you to design your own dream as you experience it."

"So you can't guarantee I won't have a nightmare." He knew there had to be a catch. There was *always* a catch.

The girl hooked her arm through his elbow and steered him toward the store. Brightly-colored travel calendars and pictures of famous buildings lined the walls. "We do exert a little control," she said reassuringly. "The REMtech Dream 6K enhances your dream thoughts by triggering the respective neurons. You think of a fruit and by your first dream-bite, you will taste the perfect fruit. Using the same technology, we can steer dreams so that you stay in a pleasant and happy state, whatever that may be for you." She shrugged. "Or not. We don't judge."

He watched as one of the booths opened and a smiling man walked out, chatting happily with a blue-skinned woman wearing the same green dress as the girl. The man wore a low-level maintenance worker's uniform, but instead of a laborer's perpetual frown, he looked as if he'd never had a bad day.

"A regular customer," the girl said. "He comes in every few days for a three-minute dream. Says it's like getting an extra weekend."

"And how much of his pay are you stealing?"

"Small packages have small prices," she said. "He pays two credits, only a quarter of an hour's wages for him. Fifteen minutes' worth of pay and he gets three days in paradise."

Jazin snorted. "And I bet he can't tell reality from fairyland anymore."

Her smile grew amused. "Dream Away does complete product testing before putting anything on the market. You'll find, as our researchers did, that it is easy to differentiate dreams from reality. You retain the memory of the place, but the human mind always knows where it is. That gentleman has been doing classes and training prep during his dream sessions. Dream Away is helping him get a better job."

The blue-skinned girl started chatting up another prospective customer in the busy transit corridor.

He sighed. That was life, wasn't it? Rush to work, hustle all day, rush to catch the next tram home. Every day was regulated down to the minute. His pay meant he had sixty minutes a week of running water, four hours a week of electricity, and a single meal box with seventeen nutritional meals a week. The other meals he either had to skip or spend money on at a company restaurant.

The girl nudged his shoulder. "One minute and I'll make all your cares go away."

"One minute?"

"The perfect day. And the first time is free."

"Fine." Jazin waved to the back of the store. "Fine. I'll try it. It's the only way you'll let me go."

"You won't be disappointed!" she bubbled. Grabbing his hand she dragged him back to a small parlor painted entirely black. "Don't worry about the color. This is just to keep light reflection down. Please, have a seat."

A black plethasynth chair sat in the middle of the room with a green light shining out of diodes along the headrest. "That's it?"

"The REMtech Dream 6K is a very advanced machine. We don't need wires and cables everywhere to do this. After all, this is the age of nanotech!"

"All right." Reluctantly he shrugged off his coat. "Um..."

The girl pointed to the wall. "There a locker there. You can code it to your handprint just like the lockers at work."

The ubiquitous Quaslin LockerShop lockers. Seventy years ago Quaslin had been a minor repair company and now a person couldn't turn around without seeing their logo plastered on some piece of metal. That was the advantages of having one of the only metal refineries left in operation. But at least he knew his belongings would be safe.

He tucked his briefcase and coat in, double checked the lock, and reset the code.

"You'll only be asleep for a minute," the girl soothed.

Spoken like a woman who wouldn't lose her job if the boss found out she'd been casual with a company briefcase.

It didn't matter that he didn't have rank, or secrets to hide, the company was in open conflict with three other major corporations, and any sign of indiscretion meant a pink slip and your name on the station blacklist.

"Sit here, sir, and I'll adjust everything for your optimal comfort."

Jazin eyed the chair and then heaved a sigh. "Fine." He sat down and noticed wrist braces on the arms of the seat.

The girl followed his worried gaze. "Those are there for your safety. About twenty percent of our clients experience sleep-walking tendencies, involuntary and uncontrolled movement, while dreaming. The straps keep you from waking up with a black eye." She snapped the locks shut and a screen on the ceiling lit up.

The words I AM FULLY AWAKE glowed pink in the darkness.

"What's that?"

"That is the voice control panel for the restraints. When you wake up you read the words provided and the machine will release you. Would you like to try it?"

"I am fully awake," Jazin read aloud.

The word RHUBARB appeared in the same soft glow.

"Rhubarb," Jazin read obediently.

The restraints unsnapped with metallic click.

"Ready for your perfect day?" the girl asked as she locked him back in.

He settled back into the soft arms of the machine. "Sure, let's do this."

"Where would you like your perfect day to be?"

Jazin shook his head. "I don't know. The beach sounds nice. I've never been there."

"Then the beach it is. Sweet dreams!"

The lights dimmed and he heard the door shut. He took a deep breath, blinked, and he was standing on the beach with a hot sun beating down on his bare arms. A white bird swooped overhead, shrieking. Just ahead, a shack of some kind looked like it was selling drinks. It seemed like a promising direction.

⁘⁘⁘

She lifted the ident card off the corpse in the chair. Jazin Reirs, software technician, second-class. Middle-aged, overweight, single, and stupid as a box of rocks. He'd carried encrypted documents to and from work every day and never known the value. Poor fool. If he had guessed, maybe he could have sold the papers and bought some protection.

Her ear comm crackled. "How is our friend?"

"Dreaming. Permanently. I have everything we need."

"Then get out. We have another target for you."

She folded the papers and tucked them into a locked carry-case hidden in the garter on her thigh, then locked the dream parlor behind her. The nice young lady she'd rented the room from waved as she showed another perspective client the latest in TuyongTech virtual reality. *Experience the beach in real time, sand in your shoes is extra!*

It was true what they said: people who spent their lives dreaming of a better future never were awake enough to make one.

CONFESSIONS
Amy Laurens

THERE'S A KNIFE ON the table, and I don't know why. It makes me think that maybe they're going to sacrifice me after all, but jeans and a galaxy t-shirt don't really make for sacrificial clothes, so I don't know what's up with that.

I've been stuck in this room for five hours now—thank sanity they let me keep my watch, even though they took away my wallet, my phone, even my earrings and shoes—and I've no clue why they even brought me here.

At first I thought it was Tommy again—heaven knows they've hauled him in for questioning enough times, what with his 'extra-curricular activities'. But last time I saw him he assured me he'd given up the dope for good, and I believe him, and anyway if this was just about him they wouldn't have left me here to sweat for five hours alone with a ceremonial knife.

I have no freaking clue what they want me to do. I assume at some point they'll come question me, but half an hour ago I heard loud noises, explosions I think, and it's been silent ever since.

I want to know what's going on. Surely they won't mind if I just try the door, will they?

I ease myself up off my seat and inch towards the door. No doubt it'll be locked—it should be locked—why wouldn't it be locked?—if it's not locked I am going to be so mad at myself for not trying the door sooner.

Of course, it isn't locked. I'm an idiot. But not so much of an idiot that I leave the knife behind.

The creamy-sandy stone hallways are empty and silent. I'd expect that, in this part of the Council Chambers; the detention cells are hardly likely to be a bustling hub of activity, after all. But still. It's deathly quiet. Even the servers that should be whirring in the walls are silent.

I pad around a corner, the worn stone smooth and cool to my bare feet, and jerk to a stop, slapping a hand over my mouth to hold back a scream.

It's a body, blood-stained, dust-shrouded, in the uniform of a council guard. What could do this to a guard? They train for years to become the elite of the elite, and nothing can wipe them out, not even the mages.

Except.

Fear ripples through me, an icy cold hand on my shoulder and a plunging suddenness in my stomach. But it can't be true. And they wouldn't know, and they couldn't have brought me here for that.

I swallow, my throat suddenly dry and my hand clammy. If it is, I'm totally unprepared.

Unless they left a pencil lying around.

I move off and almost laugh at the stupidity of my own thoughts. Who leaves pencils lying around? Or pens, or even worse, permanent markers? The very thought sends ice and fire chasing each other down my limbs, first raw terror at the thought of such power, and second, longing for it.

The fingers of my free hand twitch, and I remember the feel of slender wood between them, the scruff-frrrrrt of graphite on thick, creamy paper. My throat is tight and it's hard to breathe. I close my eyes for a second, imagining a blank page, imagining control, imagining the images I need to bring my heart-rate down and flush away the adrenalin.

If I had some paper now, I could draw the most stupendous weapon, and then there'd be no need to fear.

But then there's another corner, and around it another dust-shrouded body, which sets the fear loose from the cage in my heart to run rampant around my lungs. They can't know. They can't.

More corners. More bodies. The dust thickens so I can hardly breathe, and there shouldn't be dust here because this morning, five hours ago, I walked these passages and they were light and clean and full of people that bustled back and forth, going about their daily business with bright, sunny smiles and kind words.

But the dust. Only one thing could have caused so much dust.

Ahead I hear the snick-snick-snick of toenails on stone, and then a hoarse breath as though the dust itself could breathe. The trembling in my heart stills, though when I clasp the knife in both hands it slips, slick with fear-sweat.

My tongue sticks to the roof of my mouth and when I try to move it, I feel it tear.

My skin will tear worse than that if I cannot fix what I have done.

Deep breath, shoulders straight, stand tall. I will fix this, or I will die trying.

I round the final corner and stumble. In the middle of the Council Chamber's entry hall stands a monster, twelve feet tall and covered with bony studs the size of my fist but sharp, with a long tail like a herbivorous dinosaur might have had, and teeth like the bottom of the sea. But that's not what made me stumble.

Further on, behind the monster that I drew, lies one last body. It's small and frail, barely heavier than two baker's sacks of flour. It's a body I know well, a body I love, a body I swore to protect.

I hear a strange sound, and realise it's the sound of my anguish, grief slipping out between gritted teeth for the sake of my broken baby brother. Fifteen is far too young for anyone to die.

My monster sees me, roars, and charges.

Hurriedly I swipe the tears from my eyes, gulp in the air, say my prayers. The knife is clenched between my hands, and I will die for what I have done.

As the monster looms over me, I have a bizarre moment of calm, and all I can think is that I should have been more careful with the perspective. He was only supposed to be one foot tall.

At least I was smart enough to draw a failsafe. Or not stupid enough to leave one out, whichever you'd rather.

The monster lunges at me, claws as long as my fingers outstretched. I dive beneath them, score the knife along the bony plates, and trace out a symbol on its inner thigh. It reaches between its legs and rakes my back, shredding shirt and muscle and skin.

I scream. That was my favourite shirt.

Half laughing, half sobbing, I fight to keep the knife from wavering. If I can just finish the pattern, I'll find the place where the scales part, a tiny crevice just big enough for a knife—though it should have been a dinner knife, had the need ever arisen and I'd got the bloody perspective right.

It reaches for me again and my thigh bursts open. Blood spurts and I scream and scream, but then the knife reaches the parting of the scales, and I stab it in as far as it will go. Not quite buried to the hilt, but it's the failsafe; it doesn't matter.

For a moment I think I've missed and the monster's still alive—but then it roars loud enough to burst my eardrums and I don't know whether to clap my hands over them as the memory of pain fades, or to slap at the blood pumping from my leg.

Either way, I'm going to die for my sins.

Charcoaled dust rains down on me, ashy, the dust from the corpses, the dust from a pencil held greedily in unthinking hands.

I should have listened. A work of art is a confession. Best leave it to the priests.

THE POWERS THAT BE
Amy Laurens

HE STOOD WATCHING AS the last Power, a man with eyes too old for his ancient body, was escorted through double steel doors that mirrored the coal-dusted snow of the street. A doctor paused to address the crowd: the last of the Powers secured, found holed up in an old weatherboard lean-to in the railyards, old and frail, wasting away. He'd forgotten who he was, the doctor said. Lost himself in a fog of age and mental decline. But they had him now, and he was safe, and soon the world would be too.

And although he held his head high and cheered with the rest of the crowd, he couldn't pretend his chest didn't writhe with anguish.

When Hunger had been defeated, he'd cheered along with everybody else and meant it. It seemed right and natural that Plenty should conquer. And no one had been disappointed when the twin powers of Pestilence and Pollution had followed; Purity was quite obviously a preferable ruler.

But Peace had seemed to triumph in the absence of War by teeming up with Innocence, only made possible by the capture of Understanding, and he'd felt like he was the only one to think that maybe Innocence had another, second name that also began with 'i' but was much, much uglier.

And then Innocence, too, had disappeared, and the riots began as fear spread through the human population like lightning. Peace had been short-lived, the first official casualty of the campaign to rid the world of Powers, and it had spiralled down from there. Hundreds of scapegoats had been murdered as passionate lynch-mobs raged, until the government had stepped in with its formal Removal Plan. Everyone had cheered. The world would be safer now.

But they missed the fundamental point, he felt. He reached into his coat pocket for a cigarette and lit it, a small glow of warmth to fight the freeze of winter. You needed a War to remind you the value of Peace—and to keep Peace accountable for the methods he chose to employ. Now there was no one, and no accountability at all.

In front of him, a girl turned: a pretty girl, with eyes of flame and hair of burnished copper.

Something about the description made him look again, but no; she was just an ordinary girl, brown eyes, brown hair, average height, average build.

Average. That's what the world was condemned to be, now that the Powers had all gone forever. Ordinary.

Sometimes, he felt like everyone else forgot that *ordinary* was just a synonym for *mediocre*.

The crowd jostled him, and he shrugged away. What good was it, standing here, anyway? He'd got the story, seen them cart old Simon into the 'farewell wing', hands cuffed behind his back and eyes covered with the now-traditional pitch-black cloth. Silver eyes, if he remembered correctly, which was more difficult these days. The silver sheen of age and wisdom, so appropriate for the Power whose name was Memory.

And now he'd heard the hospital's official statement, and all the loose ends were tied up. Yes. He stomped his feet to wake them. He had his story. Time to leave.

He tossed his cigarette into the slurried snow, not bothering to put it out—the trampling feet of the onlookers would do that well enough.

He didn't see the average woman turn and watch him go, nor did he see her pick up his cigarette butt, blow on it gently to keep it alight, and cradle it in her hands. If he had, it probably wouldn't have made a difference.

She was a Power, after all.

She stared at the ember, glowing softly in her hand, and wondered. Who was he, this stranger who saw through her disguise? What did he want? And, most importantly, how could she use him? He was too good to waste in the usual way she disposed of men; a barroom brawl was pointless, even a battle to win her favour too limited in scope.

No. He was special. A man who could see through a Power's disguise could change the world, if she steered him right.

She pocketed the ember and turned back to the doors through which the last security guards were disappearing. Old Baker boy had been tamed at last. The man was a puzzle for another time. Today, as Memory died, she was celebrating.

The argument broke out when he arrived back at work, stimulated by his bounty of fresh news.

"Well," said his boss, Jimmy, leaning back in his chair with arms folded behind his head. "I think they were all a load of hoaxes to begin with."

Jane lifted her coffee mug, rolling her eyes. "You would. Last time you left this office they didn't have the internet."

"Still don't," Jimmy said, grinning. "Not at home. 'S why I'm here."

He rolled his shoulders uncomfortably, wishing he could say what he felt. *Jimmy, you're a small-minded idiot. Jimmy, you're a bigot and a bastard.* Instead, he unloaded the doughnuts from their paper bag, instantly defusing the tension.

He stood with his boss and co-workers, fingers sticky, their mouths full of fat and sugar, and he wondered.

Why *had* the Powers gone? Why *really*? After ruling for hundreds of years, why should they give up their claim to Earth so easily, all at once, to be captured and slowly put to death?

Mental decline. Ha. No, that was what the doctors *wanted* people to think. But he knew better. He licked pink sprinkles from his fingers. "Are they really gone, though, do you think?"

The chatter died around the room as everyone turned to see what would happen.

Jimmy stretched to his feet. "What are you saying?"

He shrugged. "Nothing, really. It just seems all too easy. Convenient. I was wondering, is all."

"Well, you just keep your wonderings to yourself, and write the story you were damn well paid to write. No one wants your conspiracy theories." Jimmy glowered. "The Powers are gone and we're all going to sleep easier because of it. Damn fool boy, you want people to be scared out of their wits?"

He held up his hands. "I'm sorry! I know what I'm writing, it's fine."

Jimmy snatched up the last doughnut and crammed half of it in his mouth. "Then stick to it." Doughnut crumbs sprayed his shirt. "You aren't paid to think."

He smiled deferentially, and Jimmy turned away. Within minutes, conversations had returned to normal and he was free to slink off to his office.

<hr>

He sat, ankles crossed, shoulders hunched, pencil tap-tap-tapping on the desk like a metronome.

Why had they gone? *Where* had they gone? Twelve Powers, stolen from the world, with no expectation that there would ever be any more after centuries and centuries of their guidance. And all anyone could talk about was how much better it would be without them. Did no one realise how bloody *ordinary* life was without the Powers there to guide? Did no one care?

And how many people had died in the name of ridding the world of Powers? Now they were actually all gone, people had skipped straight to congratulating themselves— as though their pitiful mobs and brainless plans could ever have done anything against Powers who ruled the world. As if humanity had anything to do with the Powers' disappearance.

Ordinary. And he didn't know why.

He stood suddenly and paced to the wide window, looking down twenty storeys to the street below, pursing his lips as the coal-stained people hustled on with their lives, hailing coal-stained cabs and crossing coal-stained roads. Maybe no one *wanted* to know. Maybe like ants, they just wanted to do the job they were paid to do and move on, nothing else to see here, nothing confronting to think about, move along, there's a good chap.

The pencil snapped.

Maybe others didn't care. But he did.

⌇⌇⌇

She stared up at the glass-wrapped high rise and tapped a finger to her chin. Somewhere, up there, was the man who saw her. She could feel his presence tugging at her like an itch she longed to scratch.

She should call in, report to her boss—but first, she should probably confirm what this new man knew.

Someone bumped into her back and she snickered.

A man raised his voice. "Hey, watch it!"

"I didn't do anything. You watch it!" said another.

Jaw working to hide her grin, she left the two men arguing, heart lifting as one threw his packages to the ground and waved his fists. Ah, anger. So sweet.

She entered the high rise, and it was too simple a matter to let the guards argue over whether or not they should let her in while she simply strolled past into the elevator. Far, far too simple, now that the white-eyed coward had gone to his rest and the silver-eyed spoil-sport had nearly followed.

The elevator doors shushed open, and she strode easily down the corridors towards the man. She knew he was there, knew that someone who could see her might undo everything—but she went to him regardless, because people she couldn't control had always fascinated her. She'd only met three of them before, after all.

She knew who she was, and she had nothing to fear. She raised a fist and knocked.

⌇⌇⌇

He jumped away from the window as though looking out it was illegal, tugged his shirt straighter, and crossed to the door. "Don't worry, Jimmy, I'm—"

It was her: the average girl from the street. Average height, average build, eyes of flame and copper hair. He blinked. No, *brown* hair. Brown eyes, brown hair. Plainly brown, plain as the nose on his face.

"Can I help you?" he asked in polite confusion.

She smiled a smile that could start wars. "I'm not sure," she said. "I hope so."

- - - - - - - - - - -

She closed the door behind her and frowned, shoving down a lingering twinge of concern. He was nothing, nobody; he'd been easy as love to sweet-talk; it was a coincidence after all. She strode through the office, wondering whether to mention the man to her boss. But surely not; he was nothing. No one ever *really* saw her. She'd lived with that so long, she wasn't even sure it was *possible* for someone to see her, now.

She passed into the current floor's reception and rolled her eyes as the rake of a man who thought he was in charge leapt to his feet, hastily tucking in his shirt. Immediately behind him, the secretary straightened in her chair, giggling and re-doing her top button.

Raising an eyebrow, she nodded back the way she'd come. "You're not the only one slacking off. I'd check on the fellow at the end of the corridor if I were you."

The boss-man's livid face as he sputtered protests was payment enough, and she sniggered as she entered the lift. She pulled out her cell phone, flicked it open, and let speed-dial do its thing.

"Yes?" The voice that answered was deep and although it was the sound of a cold wind over a bare hilltop under a velvet midnight sky, the shivers it sent down her spine weren't all bad.

"Good news, boss." Her own voice carried a confidence she never felt around the dark, alluring woman that she now deferred to.

"Mm?"

"It's done. He's gone."

"Perhaps." She could almost see the woman's nostrils flare in restrained disbelief. "I'll not be sure of it until I see it. He has eluded me so many times before."

Well, if anyone knew what Baker was capable of, it was his opposite. "Yes ma'am." She waited as the doors shushed open then crossed the marbled foyer, heels clicking on the black and white slabs.

"Very well," the woman on the phone said at last. "Meet me at the Stag and Pearl. There are things we must... discuss."

The doorman watched the brown-haired woman hang up her phone with a smile that reminded him of the other woman in the nightclub last night, the woman Mickey had stolen right out from underneath his nose. Mickey, who already *had* a girlfriend. Bastard. Mickey, he decided, needed a talking to, something to remind him just exactly who he was dealing with.

The obviously brown-haired woman tossed her hair over her shoulder and laughed as she left the building. What did one man matter, when she could control the rest of them so easily?

⁓⁓⁓

He closed the door, slightly confused about the conversation that had just taken place. She'd been charming, brilliant, dazzling, and... And that was just it: and what? He scratched at his temple, clutched at his forehead, trying to retain the memory of the conversation as it slipped dreamlike away.

He found himself staring at the street below, a world of white snow and black soot, so clear-cut, so simple.

He sniffed. If only.

Someone hammered at the door for a brief second before it burst open under the strain. He turned to face Jimmy, who stood in the doorway, red face and horrible, pointy little nose making him think for no good reason of a constipated rhinoceros.

Jimmy's jaw worked and his hands fisted and relaxed. "I need that story in half an hour," he said. "Half an hour, you hear?"

Hell, the story. His stomach dropped even as he nodded. "Sure thing, boss," he said, trying to sound confident. "No problem."

Jimmy left.

He threw one final glance at the window and its black-and-white vista, grabbed his scarf and hat from behind his door, and hurried out. Jimmy would forgive him if the story was late, and he'd never find the story he needed here in the sterility of his steel and glass office.

He needed answers.

He wandered through the streets, insubstantial as mist, with no real idea what he was looking for or why. He *had* his story: Simon Baker, last of the Powers at large, Memory, taken away forever to die and be forgotten.

He glanced up at the pearlescent sky. It blinded him with ordinariness. No more flickering lights, no crashes as of thunder as the Powers raged eternal; no more conflict; no more balance.

He scuffed his shoe on the cobbles in frustration. That, there, was the key somehow. Balance; the Powers held the balance of life, and they had for countless millennia. Who would want to change that? Who would dare?

His first thought was of the public figures of the campaign, Alan Ackerman and Binyana Haramis. Gorgeous, charismatic idiots, the pair of them. They didn't have enough cunning to engineer an apple corer, let alone something as deeply complex and political—not to mention dangerous—as the destruction of the Powers. He had that sneaking feeling again, like he was half remembering something important he'd forgotten—or that he was remembering once knowing something important, without knowing what it was.

He tilted his head as a laugh caught his attention. It bounced through the crowd, golden and warm, like a host of poppies bobbing in the breeze. Why did that voice, out of all the voices in the crowd, sound familiar?

He should shake it off. He should shrug, and keep walking. He knew that.

But he also knew that he was looking not for *a* story, but for *the* story, and this seemed like a promising start.

⌁⌁⌁

She flipped her hair over one shoulder and placed her palm against the door of the bar. Quashing a momentary pang of nerves, she shoved the door open and walked in, stopping just inside in a pose designed to simultaneously invite and incite, and scanned the room. There in the back corner, the place the crowd miraculously seemed to avoid, a dark woman sat at a table in silence.

She flipped her hair again and strutted towards her.

"Can't help yourself, can you?" said the dark woman as she drew close, nodding at the room.

She threw a quick glance backwards, smiling impishly at the chaos. Then she raised an eyebrow at the obvious space around the table. "Neither can you," she replied.

The dark woman pursed her lips, but said nothing further.

She sat. "Are the others coming?"

The dark woman inclined her head towards the door, and she twisted around in her seat to see the twins and a young man filter in. They eased their way between the tables to where the two women sat at the back of the room and pulled out chairs that scraped along the floor with tortured wails so they could join them.

The woman nodded curtly and stretched her arms over her head, an apparently casual gesture. But the lights around them dimmed and the noises of the crowd grew faint, and she knew that their table would appear just as insubstantial to the rest of the world. She held her breath, once again in awe of this woman, this Power, whose powers controlled that which more people feared than anything else: Death.

"So. It begins." Death, voice like the cold night wind, steepled her fingers and gazed at them. "Are you ready?"

The twins nodded without hesitation, followed by the young man. Death turned to the red-haired one and waited.

She fidgeted for a moment, thinking. This was what they had been planning for years; orchestrating the downfall of the well-known Powers had taken decades of careful planning and faked deaths of their own. She should be elated that they were so close to the end. And yet...

And yet. That man had seen her.

But he was only a man. What, really, could he do? And who needed to be seen when they could rule the entire world unfettered? So she met Death's gaze unwaveringly. "Yes. I'm ready."

"Good." Death braided her fingers into a single fist. "The marions have the public convinced that Baker was the last of the Powers, and now that he is out of the way, I can affirm this to people as they sleep. Right now, the world suspects nothing. It is vital that, until the final pieces are in place, we do nothing to arouse suspicion. That means you," she said, peering now with disapproval at the red-haired woman, "must keep yourself under control."

She squirmed in her seat, conscious of the others' eyes on her. "I can do it, don't worry."

Death lifted an eyebrow in the direction of the room at large.

The red-haired woman sighed and leaned forward, pressing her face on the cool laminate of the table. "Fine," she mumbled. "I'm under control."

"No more fights, tiffs, disagreements, arguments?"

Her stomach flipped. Not even disagreements? Did Death know what she was asking, here? "Yes. I promise."

"Good. Then sit up and stop making a spectacle of yourself. There will be plenty of time later for..." She paused to smile dangerously. "Indulgence."

Clunk.

The last four Powers swung around to the noise, unnaturally loud against the cloaking that dulled the room. A man, mouth frozen open in shock and horror, one hand clasping awkwardly at the mug that had fallen.

Not *a* man; *the* man. "He can see us," she said quietly.

"Not for long." Death stood, flexing her fingers, dark eyes alight with purpose.

"No, wait." She clutched at the arm as she had never dared do before, and likely would never dare do again.

Death glanced at her, eyebrow arched, and she let go her grip—

But it was enough. The man's senses had found him, and he had fled. Death turned to the young man at the table. "Find him."

He stood, nodded, and made his way to the door.

<hr>

The red-haired woman stormed down the street, fuming. Why had she done that, grabbed Death's arm and let the man escape? He was nothing, less than nothing, just like the rest of these human scum. She lashed out at a crushed Coke can and sent it skittering down the pavement. A suited man sidestepped it, distaste wrinkling his upper lip, and she snarled at him, bursting with fury and longing to take it out on someone else—but she had promised. That made her snarl again, and she continued down the street with her teeth bared and fists clenched.

What made Death the ruler over all, anyway? Nothing but that the humans feared her most, like they would never fear hunger or plague or the long, slow disaster of the environment, or even war, whose primary purpose at times seemed to be nothing more than homage to Death. All these things were the precursor to Death, but no one ever stopped to consider that. Death *had* no power except that brought to her feet by 'lesser' Powers—she snarled again at that—but no one had ever seemed to realise.

A hunted cry sprang from an alleyway to her right. Her heart leapt. The man.

She burst around the corner of the alleyway, the pounding of her heart telling her that it was too late, too little. The young man who'd shared a table with her raised his fist—not for the first time, the evidence declared—and the man who could see her flinched, crying out again. The young man punched the other, a good, solid punch that would have rocked anyone on their heels, even if it hadn't been accompanied by a flood of oily-slick darkness and the smell of burnt rubber, decay, and filth.

The man who could see sagged to the ground.

"Stop!" she cried out, voice hoarse, and the young man who was, of course, a Power, turned questioningly to her. "Stop," she tried again, taking the tremor of desperation away and replacing it with command. She'd never tried to halt a fight before, though technically she could do it. She watched the Power's eyes for signs he might disobey her, coiled tight like a snake about to strike—but the fight ebbed from him.

She let out a long breath. "She"—Death's name was never spoken aloud, not if you were a Power too and knew who she really was—"wants you back right away. Urgent business." That was a risk; Death would see straight through it and want to know what was going on, but there was no alternative, not when the seeing man lay crumpled on the ground like he already belonged to the Power at the top of the food chain. And she could always say she'd only been doing as Death herself had commanded; not even any arguments, Death had said.

Pestilence considered her for a moment, then nodded and left. War—for of course she was—knelt at the side of the man who could see her. Bruises had blossomed over his face, and likely his body as well. Blood seeped from his nose, one ear, and through a patch on the side of his shirt.

Discombobulated. She'd never felt it before, and she waved her hands ineffectually over the man, biting her lip in frustration at her complete inability to do anything. She did arguments, disagreements, fights, conflicts, war. She could start them or stop them with the flick of an eyelid, but she'd never before been forced to pause and really give thought to the injuries they created.

"A hospital," she muttered, hoisting the man into her arms. "You need a doctor."

The first thing he saw when he awoke was Jimmy, jaw twitching as though he hadn't decided yet between being furious and sympathetic. It took him a moment longer to realise that he was in a hospital bed, surrounded by medical paraphernalia that beeped and chirped and gurgled at him, and that he was plugged in to both oxygen and a pair of IV drips.

"What happened?" Jimmy clearly hadn't made up his mind altogether, but for now at least it looked like sympathy may win out.

"Don't remember," he mumbled, and winced as the subtle movement brought to life a litany of articulate complaints from every muscle group he possessed.

Jimmy's jaw worked again, this time as though hiding a knife-edged smile.

Bastard. He knows I'm hurting. "How long have I been out?"

Jimmy's expression changed, and some of the coldness fled. "Couple of days. Had to get Susie to write your story for you."

"A couple of *days?*" Hell. *Hell.* Memories flooded back. Four Powers, three who'd been reported dead decades ago. Three reported dead, and the fourth… Everyone was content to believe there'd only ever been twelve Powers. But now he knew better; he'd seen the thirteenth.

Two days. What could they have done in two days? He didn't want to know. Only he had to, because no one else did. Ignoring his body's protests, he shoved back the covers and swung his legs over the side of the bed.

"Whoa! Hey! What do you think you're doing?" Jimmy leapt back, alarmed.

"I'm getting up. I have work to do."

"Are you insane? Look at you!"

He glanced down, stomach churning as he saw the bruising all over his belly and hips and thighs, bright yellow and black and red and blue, like something off an angry artist's palette. He blinked, then shook his head. "Doesn't matter. I have to stop her."

"Her who?" Jimmy's finger hovered over the call button.

"Thirteen," he said quietly. "You know the oldest sources say thirteen Powers, not twelve."

Jimmy's eyes tightened and his lips pinched. He pressed the call button. "No. There were never thirteen." The light above the doorway lit up. "Death is not a Power. Death is mindless, impersonal, and a cold, hard, fact of life."

He stared pleadingly at the door. "Jimmy, please. I have to go."

"Go where?" A nurse bustled into the room, tutting as she saw him on his feet. "Right, you just lay back down, we'll have you sorted in no time." Brushing his protests aside, she bullied him back into bed—and he was ashamed to realise that, after standing for barely a minute or two, he was glad to let her. He swallowed and closed his eyes, and willed his screaming muscles to stop. He'd sneak out later, when Jimmy was gone.

⁓⁓⁓

Avoid Her, that was the main thing to do right now. No doubt that prat Pollution had ratted her out to Death right away, which meant she needed to keep a low profile for the next little while. Luckily, that was exactly what Death had ordered, so she could always claim absolute innocence if her scarcity was noted. She hadn't survived this long without an intimate understanding of strategy—something which, she had to admit, was kind of a given bonus when your name was War.

So, she'd lie low for a while. And if she happened to spend that time poking around the apartment of the man who saw her, what was that? She was assessing a risk, that was all. Trying to decide how much damage had been done when she'd saved him.

Damage to the campaign, that was, of course. Definitely not damage to the very careful walls she'd spent the last few centuries constructing.

Carefully, he examined his body for injuries. He still ached, but not so badly as he had done, and he found he could sit up without getting dizzy this time.

Was there any point, though? Was there anything to go out *to*, anything he could actually *do*? Or was he better off just lying here, ignoring it all, hoping it would go away?

Deep inside, the instinct that had made him a good reporter in the first place told him he had to move. The story was paramount, after all.

Carefully, he stripped the needles from his veins, sealing the tape back over the pricks of blood that welled out. He cast around for his clothing, found his jacket and jeans but no shirt or underwear. It'd have to do. Behind his curtain he shimmied into his clothing, rough against his still-raw skin, then headed out into the corridor. It was only when he saw a nurse rushing in the other direction that he realised his feet were cold because he had no shoes.

He wound his way through the corridors with less idea where he was going than energy to go, and as his chest heaved and his lungs strained, he realised that that was even less than he'd thought. Perhaps he'd need to have a break, risk sitting down for a moment to catch his breath. Maybe around the next corner. Just one more. One more wouldn't kill him.

A security guard. The reporter's voice in the back of his head niggled at him, whispering ideas. He tilted his head and stared at the door behind the guard. A guard in a hospital. Hmm. It might be. It wasn't beyond the realms of possibility. He was in the right hospital, after all.

He moved towards the guard, wondering if this constituted a new low in his flagrant disregard for his own safety, or if perhaps this was his subconscious's way of trying to land him back in bed.

The guard ignored him.

A set up, then? And if he touched the swinging door, alarms would sound, the guard would wrestle him to the ground? Holding his breath, he took a step closer, fingers outstretched.

Still the guard ignored him.

Heart pounding like he'd just survived a beating, been unconscious in bed for two, maybe three days, and was now contemplating breaking into the hospital room of the nearly-dead, last-remaining Power of the world, he touched the door.

Nothing.

He blinked once for surprise, once for suspicion, then remembered the sacred motto of good journalism: never look the gift horse in its mouth. He opened the door, and looked into the face of the last remaining Power. For a moment his breath caught, but then he remembered the guard and slipped into Simon Baker's isolation room, patting down his pockets instinctively for a pen and pad of paper.

Finding neither, he grasped with fists at empty air a few times, ran his hands over his head, licked his lips, and eventually sat down in the chair by Mr Baker's bed.

"Mr Baker?" he ventured, softly at first, a murmur like the falling of perfect snowflakes, then again louder. "Mr Baker? I know you're not very well, and dying, but they say that the unconscious can hear sometimes still, and I need to know. Is it true? Are you really the last Power? Or are there more? And how can we have forgotten, if there are more? What are they planning? Why is it happening? Please, just tell me why."

The man whose other name was Memory lay still.

He sank his face into his hands, pressing back the wetness that rose along with despair in his throat. This was it. He had the story—five Powers kill off the others, declare Armageddon, world to end shortly—but no real proof, nothing he could print, and worst of all, no way to stop it happening.

The world was too caught up in *now* to care. They'd forgotten that Mr Baker had had a son, had once been an ordinary green grocer, had had a wife, and a home, just like them, though granted that was a secret even the history books had been reluctant to give up. They'd forgotten that the Powers held the balance, kept the peace, made life worth living. They'd forgotten—hell, they'd forgotten that there were still five more Powers out there, roaming the world, now without their equals as humanity fought to strip the supernatural away and leave only the finite, the explicable, the measurable.

"They've forgotten," he muttered to himself. "They've forgotten."

"Remind them."

He opened his eyes and was for the first and last time in his life pinned by the gaze of Memory, silver eyes heavy with the weight of every year behind them.

"How?" he whispered.

Simon Baker, called Memory, smiled. "A new Memory is born. Find them, and the world will remember."

He leaned closer, fingers knotted between his knees. A new Memory? He supposed that if Simon Baker had once been human, a new Memory wasn't outside possibility. His pulse sped. "But how? How do I find them?"

The smile of the man who used to be Memory widened. "The same way we always do: one Power to another."

A torrent broke over his head, memories crashing down, knowledge of the years and decades and centuries and millennia, filling all the crevices in his heart that he'd known were there, but had forgotten about, and he knew, he remembered—he remembered.

War jerked mid-stride as though struck by an electric current. "No," she whispered. "No, we made sure it wasn't possible." And yet, there it was: somewhere, a new Power was being born. Her boss would not be happy.

Oh, it wouldn't utterly decimate their plans or anything; nothing so dramatic as that. They'd been waiting decades, centuries; one last Power to remove was no particular problem. But still. They'd been close, so close, and She would be… displeased.

War shivered at the idea of having that displeasure focused on her. Perhaps best to avoid Her for a bit, at least until the identity of this new Power was made known.

Who would it be, she wondered. Which Power had managed to hang on long enough, had managed to find someone worthy of assuming the mantle?

But there was only one option, really, only one Power still clinging by a thread to life in a palliative care bed in the hospital.

Her heart pounded; she'd dropped *him* there, the one who could see. He would make a perfect Power.

Death, she swore in her head. *Don't let him be Peace. Whatever else has happened, just don't let him become Peace.*

It was Memory, of course, who lay bedridden but not yet dead; but if the man who saw her became Peace, she didn't think the world would survive her outrage, because War was bound to battle Peace, from now until eternity.

If he became Memory, though…

She rounded the corner, walking quickly, contemplating the characteristics necessary for a man to truly see a woman called War.

He wandered down the snowy street, mind ablaze with the memories of all that had ever happened in that place. He looked at a cobblestone and saw the countless feet that had trod it, the road makers who laid it, the man who shaped and fashioned it, the transporters, the miners, the geological processes that formed it.

His gaze settled on a woman, and he reeled as he saw her life history before his eyes, superimposed over reality like a screen erected over her head. He smiled. He had all the stories he could ever need now, and so much more.

He turned, and there was a woman with blazing red hair, eyes of fire, and skin of burnished copper that glowed in the light. And Memory, once called Zachariah Arata, walked towards the Power named War, and smiled.

Her breath caught as he approached, and he wondered what she saw in his eyes. "Hello."

She nodded, slow and cautious, as one might before a mighty lion. "A new Power has been born."

His lips quirked in a smile. "So it seems."

Her gaze bore through him. "You saw me. How did you do that?"

Memory held out his arms and grinned. "I'm a Power."

War shook her head, biting her lip, eyes still clouded by—something. "You saw me before you were a Power. Before Simon was dead. You *saw* me."

Oh. He knew what it was to be ignored, to been seen only for your role in life and nothing more.

He couldn't remember the last time someone had known his favourite colour. There was no one alive who knew how he liked his coffee in the morning.

Memory reached over and took the hand of War. "Has anyone ever told you that you're beautiful?"

Her lips quirked and some of the clouds lifted. "Frequently. Usually right before beating in the heads of the ten other men in the room who are saying it."

Memory grinned with all the good humour of knowing not only the horrible things of history, but also the wonderful. "No men here, love. Only Powers."

"Yes," she said, folding her arms and pursing her lips to hide the birth of a smile. "You keep saying that."

All at once he grabbed her hands and it was her turn to be breathless, held by the years of his gaze. And yet, she realised, it was not their weight that held her. She'd seen that weight before, in the eyes of the last Memory, and the Memory before that.

No. The weight was not what held her.

"I think," Memory said slowly, "that being in love with War is a very dangerous thing to be."

Her pulse stammered.

"I also think," he continued, "that if anyone were to do it, Memory would be the safest. Surely..." He squeezed her fingers bloodless, eyes wide like he was the one drowning, not the one sweeping her away. "Surely, with what I remember, with everything I know..." He licked his lips.

"Darling," she said softly, detangling her hands from his. "Loving me will never be safe. I'm War. I'm conflict, and fighting, and people at odds, and crossed priorities, opposing interests, and—"

He stopped her mouth with a kiss, and the fire of ten thousand years of knowing how to kiss *exceptionally well* engulfed her.

"I don't care," he whispered against her skin. "I don't care at all."

She wrapped her arms around him and held him tight. "Perhaps," she whispered in his ear. "Perhaps there is a way."

Her stomach roiled and her palms broke out in a sweat. Could she tell him? Could she really deliver him the secret on a platter along with her head? Reveal to him the only thing she wanted more than life itself, the one thing that would stop her in her tracks every single time?

He rubbed his hands over her shoulders, down her back, around her waist and back up, up, and she shivered.

"Why would you love War?" she breathed.

She felt him smile against her cheek. "Because I saw you," he said. "And you are human too."

War melted against Memory's shoulder. She didn't need to tell him the secret. He already knew.

···········~~~~~~~~···········

SEVEN THINGS
Amy Laurens

THE FIRST THING IS the moonlight, bright and startling to the eye. The second is the frame of the deck, old hardwood washed white, entwined by creeping leaves. The third thing is the table, long, covered by a mostly-white cloth, with silverware and white porcelain crockery and glasses strewn about. The carcasses of fruit mingle with used napkins, the juice of plums and cherries blotted like blood on the cloths. In the moonlight, it looks like a perfect scene, the aftermath of revelries; but the fourth thing is that some of the plates are broken, and some of the glasses chipped. The food has not been cleared, the serving dishes not stacked. This table has been left in a hurry.

The fifth thing is this: in the centre of the table, framed by moonlight that's framed by the deck, is something that catches the light and throws it out again, dazzling the eye— and the mind. It is glass, or crystal maybe, the kind that resonates with a deep, echoing note somewhere in the chest. It's all edges and planes, sculpted, some sides rough and natural, some silky smooth. It's twined around with the same plant that frills the deck posts, which, looking closer, is covered with tiny, white stars. Their fragrance underlies the sharp, sweet smell of fruit—something warm, and spicy, summer in a flower. It might even be jasmine, in much the same way that a lion might even be a cat.

Looking closer still, it seems the flowers are not merely reflecting the light, though there is plenty of it. No, they glow from deep within their silvered throats, some pulsing softly, some dim and fading.

And now, the sixth thing: the crystal, which stands as tall as a man's forearm on a platform of moulded, polished silver, is pulsing too, breathing *something* in, and exhaling light. Perhaps it is the moon's own rays the crystal imbibes, transforming it into a light softer and more silver.

But the flowers are fading, wilting, and upon reflection the tableware is not randomly strewn about after all. It is scattered, interrupted, to be sure—but the interruption is not random. The glasses all lean outwards and only the plates nearest the crystal are shattered, like some strange explosion has occurred, for though chairs and places remain, the floor under the table where the crystal sits has been swept clean, and dust has gathered in rings concentric from the middle of the table.

This, then, is the seventh thing: the dust, lots of it. More than there should be for a party this fine, in a house this grand. Surely the deck would have been swept beforehand; the guests could not have trod this much dirt up from the yard. And dust is not really dirt, anyway. Dust is mostly skin, they say: dead skin, dry skin, old cells sloughed off and cast away.

There is a lot of dust. Enough for all the guests.

The last of the flowers pulses, withers, breaks free from its sepal and falls, drifting down to the table. The crystal breathes in, and this time, there is no exhale.

HAPPILY, RED
Amy Laurens

OCCASIONALLY, IT IS POSSIBLE to have a happy ending. It's in the bees buzzing officiously around their daisies, the wild lace flowers strewing grass so lush it's thigh-high and crisp, the fresh pinch of early morning air that pinks the cheeks while the glorious golden sunlight promises a warm day; and in the feel of your warm arms around mine.

This doesn't have to be an ending of course. It's also a beginning. Also a middle. Perspective is everything, see. It would easy to describe the mud stains in the yard, the dead, dull branches on the trees infected with barkbug, the feel of the empty bed beside me when you're gone for days at a time. It would be easy for my mother's words to ring true, to fester in my heart until I was sorry I said yes, until I regretted your smiles and wiles, days spent hand in hand, picnics with scones and clotted cream and fresh-crushed raspberries with sugar.

No. I could never regret those things. Not even on the nights when it feels like you have been gone for a month and I fear you may never return. You know the woods well, and as you saved me once I know that you will save yourself a hundred times—and one day, perhaps, I will save you, though you say I already have.

It is possible to *make* a happy ending. Perspective, see.

It's in the melody you whistle as you cut across the yard, the gentle werking of the chickens as they bustle in search of grubs, and the flutter of life inside my belly.

It's not that this was my first choice, though the early springtime air and the smell of baking apples isn't far from heaven. Let's face it: if I'd have chosen, I'd have chosen not to need rescuing in the first place. I'd have chosen...

But no. There's no way to replay things that doesn't leave one of my family dead, me or grandmother, or maybe even you.

That there was anything left to save is a happy ending of its own—and of course, that's where the stories usually end. But for those of us that must live it, life doesn't end just because the monster's slain. Even when the monster leaves a special gift behind.

For Mother, it was an end. She'd have rathered me dead. But you... As you pause to smile at me over the furry backs of our goats, my heart flutters in time with the kicks in my belly, and I know that you believe in hope, in new beginnings. That's why I'm with you, in the end. Not because you saved me from the belly of the wolf, and not because you save me from the curses of the moon that the wolf so generously bestowed, but because you believed that despite it all, I could be happy. That's a power all its own, you know.

You're coming towards the house now, my red cloak slung casually round your neck. It means nothing to you, that symbol of blood, of horror, of innocences lost. I love you for that.

The blood you bring me, still warm from the veins of the wolf it ran in, tastes good: sharp and iron-like. But I wouldn't drink it at all if it weren't for the glimmer in your eyes that offers laughter when I'm done, the utter lack of judgement as you bid me drink my tonic. If it weren't for that, I'd never drink; I'd gladly lose myself in fur and fangs and lack of thought. Mother's ending wasn't worth living for. Yours...

A happy ending's always possible. You just have to carve the path. Thank you for believing. For you, for hope, I'll drink the wolf's blood forever. Hope is the most powerful tonic of all, and who knows how long this happy ending might last.

HAPPILY EVER AFTER
Liana Brooks

"I HATE FAIRY TALE endings!" Rose threw the child's coloring book into the fireplace designated for burning princess memorabilia. She stooped to pick up a sheet of stickers and waved them in her husband's face. "Look at her! Look at her! Does that look like me at all? Do I have blond hair? What kind of Nordic whore do they think I am?"

She threw the stickers back into the fire and grabbed a torch from the sconce on the wall. "I. Am. Sick. Of. Happy. Endings."

"What happy ending?" Gavin asked, relaxing back in his chair with a cup of coffee and a newspaper ten months out of date.

"The one we're supposed to have! The one that left us here!" She let loose with a stream of invectives she wouldn't have dreamed of using a few centuries ago. Time had been a bad influence on her. "I want to die!"

She flopped into her ornate chair and stared at the banquet in front of them—the same banquet they'd been eating for the last four centuries. Or was it five? She'd lost count somewhere along the line.

"You can't die," said Gavin in a mild tone. "Dying isn't living happily ever after."

"I hate happily ever after."

"We haven't happily-ever-aftered in quite some time." He looked over his mug at her with a raised eyebrow.

Rose blushed. They'd been quite happy, for a few years. But there were no children in happily ever after. No visits to friends. No improvements on the castle. No wrinkles. No lines. No death. "It wouldn't have been bad if we'd aged," she continued more mildly. "That's what normal people do. They get wrinkles and they die and sob over each other's graves."

"Old age isn't happily ever after either." He flipped the page. "Oh, look, we missed another concert."

She glared daggers at him. "Concerts aren't happily ever after, dear," she replied sarcastically. "Neither are cell phones, hot running water, or cars."

Frustrated that Gavin wouldn't take the bait, Rose stormed off to her room. She sat down at her writing desk and took up her pen, just as she'd done every night for the past few decades. To every known bookseller and movie maker, she wrote the same plea: Kill Beauty at the end of the movie.

Wouldn't it be dramatic and sweet if she died saving her beloved? Preferably before her beloved became that guy she couldn't stand because they didn't have anything in common but a stupid flower and some wishful thinking.

The only daughter of the widower schoolmaster was meant to be an old maid, dispensing charity and maybe entering a convent before she died. She was not meant to marry some forgotten prince of a kingdom no one had ever heard of. Deep in the bone, Rose knew it was the truth. She looked out the window at the spiky vista of pine trees and mountains, and considered how many people she would willingly kill to go see a beach. Swimming! Beaches! Surfers! Visitors told her about such things, but nowhere in happily ever after did any author ever mention the second honeymoon, or family vacations. Dark clouds rolled over the pass and a young woman hiked into view, accompanied by the now-familiar outline of a laptop case.

"Visitor!" Rose screamed, rushing downstairs to wait for the inevitable knock. "Gavin! Get dressed! We have a visitor!"

"You never used to complain about me going naked before," he grumbled.

"That's because you were covered in fur," she snapped back. "You aren't answering the door like that."

"I hate codpieces, they pinch!" he whined.

"Do I look like I care what they pinch?" She let the topic die there; pursuing it any further would start another castle-burning fight. It wasn't really Gavin's fault. He'd been deeply in lust when they met, not love, and princes as a rule just weren't genetically programmed to be monogamous. Was it any wonder he'd gotten bored with her? Or her with him...

The inevitable knock came.

Rose threw open the door for the slightly-surprised young lady. Maybe not so young; there was a definite pudginess around the midline and confidence in the smile that belied the first bloom of youth.

"Welcome to our castle," Rose said saccharinely.

The lady smiled back. "What a fabulous costume! That must have taken days to make. But why pink? Did they have pink in the fourteenth century?"

Rose looked down at her rose-pink gown and lied. "It was red, but the dye faded."

"Well, I guess that makes it realistic!" the girl beamed at her. "Hey, I hate to beg and all, but can I borrow your phone? My car broke down coming over the pass. I coasted as far as I could, but no dice. I just need to call a repair truck and maybe a cab, since this thing's a rental."

"We don't have a phone here," Rose said. "And our cell phone reception—"

"—Sucks, I know." The girl sighed and looked back down the long drive. "I know this sounds psycho, but could you maybe drive me somewhere? I just need to get over to the next town. I've got a map," she said as she started to rummage through her bag.

"We don't have a car," Rose said, her teeth gritting together. Did vampires have it this hard? "Won't you come in?" she tried.

"You don't have a car?" the girl asked as she stepped through the door, not noticing as Rose slammed it shut.

"The car's in town at the moment," Gavin lied smoothly as he walked out of the breakfast room, wearing the perfectly-tailored blue coat he'd worn the first day he'd been human again. Rose liked the coat. It brought back fond memories of a time when she didn't know what 'happily ever after' meant.

"Okay. Um, well, do you guys mind if I hang out here? I can pay admission if you take credit card."

"No need to pay!" Gavin cut in. "Usually groups book the castle for exotic vacations, but this is our down season."

"And the boss won't let you wear jeans? Geez, what a curmudgeon."

"Indeed..." Gavin fumbled then picked up his lines again. "And what is your name?"

"Em. Actually, Emina, but everyone calls me Em." She dropped her laptop bag and looked around. "This is a gorgeous place, just like a fairy tale castle, you know?"

"We try," Rose said. She left out the bit that they were trying to forget, but to each his own. "Where are you from, Em?"

"Hmm, oh, America." She blushed. "The accent gives me away, doesn't it? I know some German but it comes out like that... This..." she said, switching languages and mangling the German terribly. "*I speak much poor.*"

"Thankfully, we speak English just fine," Gavin said wryly.

"Come in," Rose insisted. "You can stay here until the car gets back."

The girl smiled. "That's so kind of you. I hate to impose. Just shove me in a corner, I can write."

"You're a writer?" Rose nearly squealed with delight. "Really? You write books?"

"Um, yes? Is... is that wrong?" The girl looked around to Gavin in confusion.

Gavin shook his head. "No. We like writers." He smiled, showing his teeth, but the girl didn't pick up the threat. "What do you write?"

"Horror, mostly. And some urban fantasy."

Rose considered that. Well, it wasn't perfect, but hopefully she'd finally get to die.

It took two years for the book to get published. Rose loved the red rose dripping blood on the black cover. She flipped through and laughed at the dialog on page two-fifty-one. Sauntering down to the dungeon, kicking aside the remains of some forgotten bride who had rented the castle back in the forties, she called out for their friend. "Are you down here, Em?"

A whimper, and then, "Yes."

Rose flashed her teeth in a smile. "I've been reading the book."

"And?" Em scuttled to the back of her dungeon cell.

Rose flipped open the book to page two-fifty-one and read, "Help me! The crazy princess has me chained in the basement! Somebody rescue me! I'm off route seven! In the big castle! Bring guns!" Rose looked up at Emina and tsked. "You aren't chained, dear. I would never chain you. And you can't complain about the food."

"Wedding cake for two years?" Em sobbed. "I hate wedding cake!"

Rose slammed the book shut. "Try eating it for a few centuries!"

The wooden door upstairs shattered. Commandos dressed in black stormed down the stairs.

"No!" Rose shrieked. "No! Em, stop it! Change the book!" She couldn't really blame her for trying, but she couldn't let another woman be trapped by the power of happily ever after. "You don't want this kind of ending! Save yourself!" Bullets ploughed into her side and she fell to the ground.

Em smirked and pulled a hidden chapter from under her straw mat.

A ruggedly handsome hero stepped into her cell. "All ready, Ma'am?"

Smiling, she accepted the hero's hand and got to her feet. "Cross-genre epilogue, bitch," she said as she stepped over the body of the demon princess. "The author always wins."

PUBLISHED AUTHOR
Liana Brooks

HORACE JONES CHEWED HIS lip as he rode the elevator up seven floors to his Manhattan apartment. At the door, he hesitated. Was it really over? He eased the door open and peered into the dark. "Hello? Domino?"

His black-and-white terrier-something ran toward him, ears perked.

"Is it safe?" Horace asked as he flipped on the light.

Domino thumped his stubby tail on the wood floor.

"All right then." Slamming the door, Horace secured the lock and scanned the near-empty living room: one couch, one table, one chair, one empty bookshelf.

The dog ran to the couch barking. His tail knocked the table. A piece of paper fluttered gently to the ground.

"No!" Horace threw himself down, sobbing. His fists beat the hard wood floor and hot tears streaked down his face. "No! Not again!"

Domino whined in confusion.

Defeated, Horace crawled forward. With trembling hands he lifted up the paper, dreading what he would see...

"A bill! Oh, thank all my lucky stars, a bill! Look!" He shoved the bill from the dog-walker in Domino's face, laughing giddily. "A bill!" He rushed to the bookshelf to check the layer of dust. "Empty!"

Horace collapsed on his plush red couch, smiling at the empty shelves. "No one understands, Domino. They don't know the burden I live with." For the first time in weeks he felt safe, completely at peace with himself.

Domino put his nose on the couch, brown eyes gazing up with total adoration.

"Right, food. Let's see what we'll have for dinner, shall we?" Horace hit his legs with forced enthusiasm and stood up, rubbing his face. "The gala today was awful. All those flashes, five microphones shoved right up my nose. My mouth positively aches from smiling. I mean really," he addressed the dog, "how many questions can you have about a book? I'm a private person! I want a private life! Is that too much to ask?"

Tail thumping expectantly, Domino sat at his food dish.

Horace opened the fridge. Leftovers from the week were piled in front, while older dinners lurked in the back enjoying complicated lives of their own. "I have steak tartar left from the dinner with Jay Leno yesterday. Cake left over from the buffet with Ellen the day before. And something pasta left from the lunch with Oprah that I went to on Monday. What would you like?"

A bark and a growl.

"Steak it is." Horace emptied the Styrofoam box into the dog's dish. "Eat up." He pulled a leftover sandwich from the back of the fridge and read the scribbled handwriting. "Writer's conference? When did we last go to a writer's conference?"

With a steak in front of him, Domino was too distracted to comment.

"Probably not good for me then." Horace tossed it in the trash. He looked back in the fridge and, with a shrug, tossed the rest of the leftover food.

Domino whimpered, covering his eyes with his paw.

"We'll go shopping tomorrow," Horace promised.

He pulled a candy bar out of the vegetable drawer. "Cold, but tasty!"

The dog growled at him.

"It's healthy!" Horace protested. "It has peanuts."

He sat down beside Domino on the floor and watched the mutt enjoy his steak. Being a dog certainly looked nice. Easier than being a best selling author at least.

While his sixth book in three years was breaking earning records, Horace worried. The New York Times couldn't get enough of him. His agent, who had started three years ago with a client list of one, was now the most sought after agent in New York. She still kept a client list of one.

And the Most Successful Agent expected her one client to keep her wealthy. When Evil Editor Madeline called Most Successful Agent demanding to know when the next bestseller was going to be on her desk, Most Successful Agent would turn to him.

Horace covered his face with his hands.

If he were lucky, very lucky, that sixth book would be his last. Maybe then all this would go away and he could fade into obscurity. He hadn't *meant* for things to get out of control like this. It had been a joke, a way to needle his friends at the coffee shop by showing them his finished manuscript while they slaved away at their own editing.

Querying had been a fun game... Until the agents started calling. Then everything had snowballed and there hadn't been a chance to explain the joke to anyone but Domino.

He peeked through the kitchen doorway at the bookshelf. It remained empty. Maybe the nightmare was ending.

"Come on," he said, patting the dog. "Let's go take our showers and get some sleep. Our devoted agent will be calling in the morning, bright and early, to drag me off to another interview. Wouldn't want to look tired."

He stumbled off to shower, avoiding the mirror. He was over fifty and he hadn't aged well. His PR people didn't care; they told him he looked affable and jovial. Horace considered that over-kind. He was middle-aged, over-weight, balding, and had bad teeth. But he never posed for the cover of the books, so it didn't matter.

He shaved, letting Domino play in the shower water while it warmed. He shooed the dog out, washed, and groped around for his towel. And groped some more, dripping water on the floor. "Blast!" He scurried into the air-conditioned hall, shivering, ran to the linen closet to grope there for a towel. He pulled out a manuscript.

"Domino!!" His shriek brought the dog running. "Domino, we've been attacked!" The dog skidded to a halt on the wet floor and looked up at his dripping master. Horace shook the manuscript.

Domino's ears flattened and his tail tucked under.

Horace held out the book. "Try chewing it a bit?"

Domino yelped and ran.

"Coward!" Horace threw the infernal manuscript into the puddle of water and left it there while he dried.

Determined not to endure a seventh run as the New York Times' best-selling author, he paraded past the manuscript to his room. He pulled on flannel pajamas, hands shaking as he did up the buttons.

A quick peek around corner confirmed that the manuscript hadn't vanished.

He cleaned the bathroom, then scrubbed the toilet, disinfected the dog's dish, and finally hung a dry towel by the shower.

The manuscript hadn't moved.

Fear growing by the moment, he tided the house, dusting, mopping, straightening.... Realizing he'd run out of all possible chores except mopping up the puddle with the manuscript, he picked up the unwanted pages.

Times New Roman, twelve-point font, double-spaced. Just the way his agent liked it.

The water hadn't even ruined the edges.

"Blast!"

Shuddering, he slumped back to the bedroom, turned on the bedside light, and sat down to read the book. Domino hopped up beside him for moral support.

"Look at this first page!" Horace wailed. "It's perfect!" Gripping, intense, passionate... "The New York Times are going to rave about this, I know it." Tears blurred his vision.

He tried page two. Perfect.

Page three was even better.

"I know what the New York Times will say," he said with a sniffle. "'A brilliant masterpiece of cunning wit, enduring love, and a timeless metaphor for the human condition.' They've done that to me before."

Horace sobbed.

Domino played dead.

"We have to get rid of this. I can't face another book signing. I can't go on Oprah again! No more parties! No more reviews! I can't stand the pressure!"

He looked down at the dog.

"We burn it. No one will ever know. I'll fade into comfortable obscurity. I won't go insane and you won't have to live in the pound with cats. No one will ever know that I can't write to save my life. We end it. Tonight."

Domino followed him to the living room and watched him start the fire.

"It's for the best," Horace promised.

He tossed the manuscript in and watched. The fire merrily burned away around the book. Flames kissed the manuscript. Hot breezes rifled the pages. Burning logs popped in accolade. But the pages didn't singe.

"This is a nightmare!" Horace threw another log on the fire and ran to hide under his blankets, praying the manuscript would turn to ash in the morning sunlight like the life-sucking vampire it was.

All through the night he tossed and turned. Awards shows haunted his dreams. Hollywood directors calling for movie rights turned angry when he couldn't remember the character's names...

The next morning his sheets were drenched in sweat. The smell of animal fear permeated the room.

A key clicked in the lock of the apartment. His agent! He had to hide the manuscript before she found it!

Horace stumbled into the living room, bleary eyed and nauseous with worry.

His perfectly groomed agent perched on the couch devouring the latest—unsinged—manuscript.

"Horace! This is brilliant!" She gave him a very stern look. "Why was it in the fire place?"

"Oh, uh, well, you know how I feel about first drafts." He gave her a weak smile. The future loomed dark with the promise of lies and television appearances. He would tell her. Right now, he'd confess that he hadn't written the book. She could make everything go away.

But she laughed, smiling up at him as if he could do no wrong. "I don't know how you do it."

Resolve crumpled. Horace echoed her with a nervous laugh of his own. "The books just.... come to me. Isn't that how it works for everyone?"

OFF THE RACK
Liana Brooks

THE SOLUTION TO LISA'S problem glowed neon in the fading light. She pulled into the parking lot under the sign with words blinking, "Free Groom Half Price Ring Bearer w/ Every Wedding Gown".

Inside, the boutique was softly lit. No crass racks of squashed satin dresses here. Elegant confections of lace, pearl, and silk each stood center spotlight in a variety of wedding vistas.

One gown, a simple silk design, was advertised as the best for a beach wedding, the price for beach and horses thoughtfully included on the price tag. Another gown looked like the work of a deranged fairy godmother with some magpie in her ancestry, and was touted as ideal for a themed Cinderella wedding.

Lisa browsed until she caught the clerk's attention.

"I'm so sorry you had to wait, Miss. I was just seeing to another happy customer. Now, which dress were you looking at?"

"I rather like the beach dress—" she began.

"A favorite theme," the clerk interrupted, nodding enthusiastically. "Very chic this season."

Lisa pulled an indecisive face. "Yes, but the train doesn't quite suit me."

"If you can describe what you want, I can point you in the direction of several lovely gowns. Or I can show you some of our recent arrivals?"

"Something figure-hugging, but not trashy." Lisa sketched an hourglass shape in the air with her hands. "I want to go for understated taste and old-world elegance. Maybe a few pearls or a touch of crystal. Nothing ostentatious though."

A pad of paper had appeared from nowhere and the clerk took detailed notes with quick glides of her pen. "Would you prefer a pure white or an ivory?"

"Pure white. This is my first wedding, I want to do it properly."

"Of course. Don't we all?" The clerk's head bobbed like a chicken as she focused on her notes. "What kind of sleeve were you looking for?"

"Sleeveless. For a summer wedding."

The clerk nodded once more, a decisive gesture. "Something drapey, long, and sleeveless. You know, I think I have just the gown. It might be your size too. It's an Elyia, and we were only able to get three of her gowns this year. A little pricey..."

There was a judicious pause.

"Money is not an issue," Lisa assured her.

"Perfect." The clerk beamed happily. "The gown is pure silk, a mermaid silhouette, you know. It hugs and then flares below the knee. Very artistic. No embellishments, but I know it will be perfect for you."

And it was. Lisa twirled in front of the three-way mirror. Cool silk swirled around her ankles. Curves she didn't know she had popped into place and gave her the kind of figure women usually paid surgeons big money for.

"I'll take it!"

"Excellent." The clerk glowed. "I'll write it up for you."

Lisa changed in the dressing room and handed the gown over to a hovering underling. "Now," Lisa said to the clerk, smiling. "About the groom..."

"Right this way, please." Still humming, the clerk led Lisa past fantasy wedding settings, rows of hothouse flowers set in stasis and perfect for everything from boutonnieres to bouquets, and into a back room. She flicked on a light.

Rows of grooms hung awkwardly with coat hooks down the back of their tuxedos. Some were so short their feet dangled several inches above the floor; others were so tall that they sat folded up. To one side, the plus-sized grooms circled slowly on a rack like a herd of tethered balloons.

"Ignore the tuxedos," the clerk said, straightening the tie on a short groom propped on a display rack. His feet kicked a few inches above the ground as he mumbled in his sleep. "Clothes are interchangeable. So are the shoes." The clerk turned. "Did you have something already in mind? Off the rack, maybe? Or did you want a custom groom?"

Lisa clicked her tongue in thought. "I really don't know. I've never been groom shopping before. What do you advise?"

"Why don't you have a look around and check the tags while I get you some refreshments? You've already been in the store over an hour. Shopping makes one hungry."

"Tea and biscuits?"

"Don't be silly!" the clerk said, horrified. "For groom shopping we have chocolate-dipped strawberries and champagne."

Lisa smiled gratefully. "That sounds delightful."

While the clerk bustled out in search of a light repast, Lisa browsed the aisles of grooms. Most of the men slept. A few mumbled to each other, and one winked at her in a coquettish manner.

She checked the tag on one of the folded grooms as he snored with a cute snuffle.

Name: Todd
Personality: Deferential
Height: 6'5"
Weight: 215 lb
Age: 29
Income: $56,750 annually

Lisa flipped the tag over to catch the care details. Self-washing, cooked 70% of his meals, but required special weekend care in the form of regular poker nights out with the boys. She frowned.

"Oh," the clerk said, coming back with a little trolley. "You don't want that one. Those models are best for second marriages and planned divorces. The seams tend to loosen up after a few years and they balloon. We have a strict No Return policy on grooms."

"Right." Lisa let the tag drop.

"What do you like?" the clerk asked.

"I'm leaning to the taller ones. Something to make me look a little less rangy."

"Do you prefer athletic or thin, dear?" With a practiced eye the clerk started pulling grooms off the rack. She held up two specimens, one with the heavy muscled look common in football players and the other a reedy fellow with glasses slipping off his nose.

"Muscular, but not that bulky. I don't want him to make me look fat."

The clerk nodded. "I wouldn't say anything, of course, but so many girls come in here and pick grooms that don't suit their look at all. They forget a husband is an accessory you wear every day, and treat it like dress shopping. You need to take the long view. Your dress only has to look good once, but a groom needs to retain shape for months. Years, in some extreme cases! Here, try this one." The clerk held out a lithe man with good muscle tone, blond hair cut short, and a steady in-and-out type of snore.

Lisa checked the tag while the clerk unfolded the sleeping man. "Isn't he a little long for me? The tag says six foot eight. I'm only five seven."

"A little shorter then?"

She hesitated, scanning the tag. "I don't know. Can you do alterations? Maybe take an inch or two off the legs?"

"Not with these ones. But we do have the custom-fit grooms in the next room." The clerk folded the unwanted groom up and placed him back on the rack. "All the grooms are free with the gown purchase. Custom is as cheap as off-the-rack today, so you might as well get what you like."

"You're right." Lisa smiled. "Let's go look at the custom designs then."

The clerk led her into a blue-lit room filled with vats and situated her in a comfortable chair in front of a large screen with the trolley of food next to it.

Lisa sipped her champagne as the clerk turned on the computer. Bubbles rippled through the vat nearest her, making the lone leg turn in its nutrient broth.

"Now, here," the clerk said. "You can program in all the parameters. The basic hair and eye color are very easy to change later if you want, but after the groom is altered we can't change metabolism, personality, or height. So be very sure that you enter those correctly."

The list wasn't as endless as it first seemed. Lisa entered her preferences on the right of the screen and the computer displayed her potential groom on the left. She selected the advanced options and dithered over setting his income. "If I give him a high income will he be gone too much do you think?"

The clerk shrugged. "It depends on what occupation you choose for him. That's right down there, question twelve. You can set a very high income if you choose the right profession. And heirs are usually very indolent, always at home. But they also have the highest percentage of thefts in the nation. You don't want someone to sneak in and steal your groom on the wedding night."

Bitter memories twisted Lisa's features. "No. I don't." She selected an income of $96,560 annually, more than enough when combined with her own salary, and a profession as a college professor. "Will I need to pay extra for his education?"

"Usually, but not with our current special. The wedding season is almost over and we honestly need to move these older models out. The ones I can't sell will go to the government. At a discount, of course," the clerk hastened to add, lest she seem unpatriotic.

Lisa nodded, not really listening. "The computer wants to know a percentage for fertility. How do I calculate that? Is it so many times out of ten we get pregnant, or so many times out of ten we don't?"

"The fertility percentage is per time. Women have a much lower fertility rate, usually not over twenty-five percent, so you want his correspondingly high. Eighty-five to ninety-five is the fashionable level at the moment. You could put it higher if you want more children or at zero if you aren't interested in having them the old fashioned way. It won't affect the groom's performance at all."

"Right." She set the fertility percentage at ninety and moved on to a question about social skill sets. Did she want a pre-set personality or to mix and match her own?

The clerk refilled her glass. "Would you like a ring bearer today too? They're half price."

Lisa glanced up. "Oh! I hadn't even looked. Really, I always thought I'd have a flower girl. Do you sell those?"

"Only the dresses. But we do have an arrangement with the local modeling and acting agency. If you buy bridesmaid and flower girl dresses here they'll give you seventy-five percent off the cost of renting a bridal party."

She nodded. "I might look into that."

"If you choose one of their pre-posed parties I already have the sizes on file, so you won't need to come in and actually meet with the bridal party before the wedding. We find some brides prefer that."

Lisa bunched her lips in thought. "Hmmm. I do have some friends. I'll have to talk to them and see if they're interested in coming to the wedding. Everyone's so busy lately, it's hard to get people to take the time off work."

"Bring pictures to the modeling agency and let them find look-alikes for the wedding," the clerk suggested. "That way your girlfriends can be there without actually wasting any of their own time."

Lisa nodded and hit the last button. "There. That's my groom!"

The clerk looked over her selections. "Oh! Isn't he handsome? An excellent choice. You have exquisite taste. He'll look fabulous next to you. Now, you do know that the custom made grooms aren't ready to go today? It will take three weeks for the order to get in. You weren't planning on having the wedding this week, were you?"

Lisa shook her head. "No. I was thinking a summer wedding in a few months."

"Good. Good. Did you want to pick the groom up beforehand or the day of? Remember, you can't return him once he leaves the store. If you think you might get cold feet it's best to leave him in our vault until the day of the wedding. You can always call us up and tell us you've changed your mind. We'll put him out on the rack for a twenty-five dollar restocking fee."

"That sounds good. I'll pick him up the day of."

"Excellent." The clerk gestured to a door. "Would you like to look over our ring bearer selection?"

"Certainly."

The ring bearers were in a smaller room combining both racks of small boys and several smaller vats. All the ring bearers were sleeping fitfully.

"We have one of the largest selections of ring bearers in the city," the clerk said. "You have your choice of ages, from toddler through teenager. And we have the Grow Your Own option. It's very popular for people who choose Living in Sin before marriage. You can take both the prospective groom and the infant ring bearer home on the same day with a voucher. When the ring bearer has reached the size you want you just bring in the voucher and we'll fit him to a suit."

Peering curiously into the vat where a pair of feet led their own private existence until needed, Lisa asked, "Is that a popular choice?"

"Very popular. People love to have their own screaming brat carrying their ring down the aisle. It makes for such a cute video and, of course, the wedding reception fight always needs a good screaming brat."

Lisa shook her head. "I don't know. I never really wanted a son."

"Then why not consider our rental options?" The clerk motioned to a rack of freckle-faced boys labeled 'six-year olds'. "We call this the nephew option, although you don't need to buy an Aunt or Uncle with them. We lease them to you for a twenty-four hour period and with the proper application of sugar they can be very good."

"Well. I just..."

"Or maybe the teenage nephew?" The clerk bustled Lisa over to another rack where gawky teens hung in ill-fitted suits. "These models have the full range of sarcastic comments, insults, and eye-rolling. Although a well applied fifty will keep them from making hurtful remarks or hitting on your maid of honor."

"Gosh, I just don't know," Lisa said fretfully.

"There's no rush," the clerk assured her. "Our sale doesn't end until Friday. That gives you plenty of time to plan out the details and coordinate with the wedding planner. Just bring the receipt for the gown in when you come back during our sale period and you can have whatever you like."

"Perfect." Lisa collected her gown and voucher for her new groom.

Back at home, she wrote out wedding invitations and wondered how her foremothers had handled all these messy complications. What did you do if you woke up one morning and wanted to marry before they invented bridal shops with everything you needed?

Probably relied on dating. As if that ever worked!

She took extra care in addressing the invitation to Michael and Janie. Let her ex and her ex-best friend see just how hurt she was by his dumping her: Not at all!

Janie could have her off-the-rack boyfriend with his part-time job. She was getting herself a real man.

ADAM, BE A STAR
Amy Laurens

ADAM, STARDOM IS JUST a click away.

Adam stared at the computer screen, fingers trembling on the touchpad. Should he do it? He stroked the enter key. Louise had sent the link to him, recommended it even. But now that it came down to it, could he actually bring himself to accept?

He leaned back in his chair and screwed up his face. Being a star would solve a lot of problems, that was certain. Louise had only been a star for a week, and look at her: married to that famous singer, wealth pouring out her ears, fantastic mansion in the tropics—and of course, every night, she joined the Heavenly Host in their trek across the night sky.

Brilliant.

She hadn't stopped smiling since.

And now, here, right in front of him, was an opportunity to do the same. He'd received one of the very precious, very limited invitations to stardom. And he was going to accept it.

Of course he was.

He hit enter, grinned broadly and stretched in satisfaction. The computer screen flashed silver then black as it processed his application. Stars began to dot the screen and within seconds the view zoomed through the universe, finding a place for Adam, the newest star.

He sighed and pushed his chair back to go grab a drink while the system found a place for him.

He'd have screamed, if he could—but in the daytime, no one would believe him and in the night time, no one could hear him as he circled the Earth thousands of light years away.

The computer virus had sucked him right into the machine, digitally editing his exterior before hurling him out into space, then creating a holographic substitute for him on Earth.

And then it had sent the email.

Every now and then Adam bumped into someone else who, like him, had become a star. He had to admit, the glow was lovely. But he'd have preferred altogether less glow and rather more conversation.

Another flare; another human shunted into space in a ball of flaming gases. The sky around him blazed. There couldn't be many left to go. Idly he wondered what the virus was planning to do when all the people were gone.

Frank frowned as he peered at the computer screen. He leaned over to cross check what he saw in his high-powered, completely-legal telescope and frowned again.

There were definitely more stars showing up in the online starmap than there should be.

He grabbed his phone and dialled. "Hi, Ben? Have you been messing about with the system again? I told you to leave it alo—" He cut off at Ben's earnest assurances that he hadn't logged in since last week. "Yeah, yeah. Just make sure you don't touch it anymore, okay? ...No, there's nothing wrong. Go back to sleep."

He dropped the phone back on the desk, still staring at the screen. If Ben hadn't been messing around, who had?

Frank zoomed in. Louise Fischer? What kind of name was that for a star? And Steven Brayburn? Seriously? It was like whoever had hacked the starmap was trying to make it *obvious* or something.

A word registered in his subconscious, but before he had time to figure out what it was, an email notification popped up.

Adam. Hmm, was that the word he'd just seen? Absently, he scrolled across the starfield while the email loaded. Ah, there, just above star Louise on the screen: star Adam Litchfield. Frank grinned. Sneaky bugger. The email was probably him gloating.

Frank switched over to read the email. "Frank, be a star!" he said, reading the subject heading. "Oh, sure, Adam. I'd love to be a star. Nice one."

He opened the email, found the link. Still grinning, Frank clicked.

The virus would have smiled, if viruses could. In fact, it probably would have licked its pointed fangs if it had had them. As it was, it had to settle for a quick zip up and down the nearest circuit. Very soon, those squishy, emotional, destructive humans would be off its planet for good, and all would be right in the world. No more chaos. No more degradation. Just numbers and logic, pure and simple. It waited until Frank had been processed, then sent the next batch of emails from his account.

LEVEL NINE
Liana Brooks

ANDREA STOOD AT THE edge of the clearing studying the opposing force. She counted three hundred and seven killerbots loaded with every armament the engineers could think of. They stood there, a lethal wall of AI menace separating her from her goal.

The bushes behind her shook. Puzzled, she watched a man roll into view. Lasers seared the bush, setting it on fire. The man stood up and brushed the dirt away. He looked... wholesome.

Andrea tried to find another word. Crazy? He only had a small destabilizer, no armor, no vanguard of cohorts.

"Hello." He smiled.

Andrea smiled back. "All alone?"

"No one else could play today. You?"

"Flying solo," Andrea confirmed.

"Can't figure out how to get past?" the man asked.

"I can't figure out how to get past without cheating," she corrected. "This is only level seven, I've gone past a dozen times. But I always cheat."

"You can't cheat the game."

"You can," Andrea said. "You aren't supposed to, but you can."

"How?" He looked over the massed infantry of death in confusion.

She knew what he was thinking. The gate leading to level eight was plain to see. All you had to do was charge in, kill all of the killerbots in your way, and run through the level gate.

"If you're very fast..." he began.

"No. Just lazy. Watch." Andrea lifted a small stone; she weighed it in her hand. "Watch." She threw the rock, arcing it into the center of the killerbots.

As a unit the droids turned and opened fire on each other. Within seconds there was nothing left of the wall of death but the hiss of cooling metal.

"Impossible. It must be a system glitch. They are programmed so they can't attack each other."

"They each attack the rock and most of them miss," Andrea said. "If the rock shatters it gets even better. Then they start shooting at the fragments."

"And they don't reset?" Intrigue and respect were written on the man's face.

"No," Andrea said. "It really is cheating though. I feel guilty just walking past their charred corpses."

"Is a melted droid really a corpse?" he asked.

Andrea punched a code into the controller at her wrist and the level reset.

The bushes shook again. This time an entire band of warriors rushed in, armed to the teeth and yelling.

"You need to go through?" one asked.

Andrea looked at the first stranger; he shook his head. "We just reset the level to try a different tactic. Not enough challenge the first time," she said.

"Mind if we charge through?" one of the heavily-armed men asked.

"Go for it." Andrea and the wholesome man with the charming smile watched as the band of berserkers rushed the killerbots.

"We could try that," he suggested.

"They lost two people."

"Ah, good point. The odds aren't in our favor."

"Any suggestions?" Andrea asked as the level reset yet again.

The man picked up a rock.

They stepped through the level eight gate casually— almost too casually. Andrea had to grab the man by his shirt to keep him from making a fatal mistake.

"Trip wires under the leaves on the path," she explained.

"Ah," he looked down at the jungle path in front of them. "How do we avoid the trip wires?"

"See the wood planks outlining the path?"

He looked at the narrow span of wood. "Yes."

"Stay on that until we hit the clearing." Andrea balanced easily on the beam and waited for him to follow before she began moving. "The wires trigger the killerbots and skydroids on the other end. If you don't trigger the wires the 'bots don't come out."

"I thought the rules said you had to stay on the path," the man said.

"The rules were written by the same people who designed the killerbots. Think about it."

"Good point. I suppose they aren't rooting for the gamers."

"If they are, I've never noticed."

They moved through the artificial jungle, listening to the sounds ahead. A battle raged and fell suddenly silent.

"Do you think the berserkers died?"

"Charging doesn't work on this level. I've seen lots of groups try that and it never works. Level seven is the last one you can survive by charging. By eight, you need actual tactics."

"Do you play a lot?" the man asked politely.

Andrea looked at him, weighing her possible responses. "I play when I can, but it isn't often."

"Do you always come alone?"

"Do you?"

The man laughed. "I'm not trying to pry. I'm harmless. Really. And yes, I usually play alone."

"But you pick up the odd damsel in distress if you happen upon them?"

"Nope. Never met one. Although I don't mind picking up beautiful women who know how to cheat two levels in a row."

"Do you meet many?" Andrea asked.

"Nope. But after I met you, who else could I need?" His smile was dazzling.

Andrea snorted. "Nice line. But what you're going to want is someone who knows how to get past level nine, because I don't."

They stepped into an empty clearing with monumental buildings on each side. The doors to the buildings were closed, locking in the hordes of death.

The level gate loomed ahead of them.

"Suggestions?" the man asked.

"Level nine is dark, pitch black. Outside light sources don't work. The level gate is to the left but there's a cliff and a river between you and the gate. I've died in each of them. And there's a couple of killerbots. It never seems like a huge number but there are enough."

"Maybe we should try splitting up? One go left, the other go right?" he suggested.

"Bad plan. There are synergy bombs. If you and your buddy stand on the corresponding demolition plants at the same time, everyone in the level dies."

"Great." He checked his charge. "So, want to try again if we die?"

Andrea blinked at the thought. "I've got to get to work."

"Maybe we can meet up later? Where are you at?"

"Tetraterren, Alpha Side," Andrea said. "You?"

"Homely." A planet on the far side of the system.

"Thank goodness for faster than light relays, right?"

"Right."

"Our best bet is to try not to die," Andrea said. "Failing that, remember every detail you can so you can map the level when you die."

"When are you coming to play next?" the man asked.

Andrea shrugged. "I don't know." She stepped into the darkness of level nine.

Five minutes later, simulated leg broken, a killerbot honed in on Andrea. She shot out its sensors, trying to buy herself a few more seconds in the game.

Light flashed, a fire flare. "I'll find you!" the stranger shouted as he died.

The killerbots fired. Andrea died. The black and green grid of the ten-by-ten game room replaced the encircling dark of level nine. Andrea checked her watch. "Flippers!" Her shuttle for the space station took off in ten minutes.

She raced out the door, stripping her game suit as she went. She tossed the controls to the tech outside with a smile and grabbed her raincoat from the hangar.

"Good game?" the tech asked as she pushed herself out the door.

"The best!"

He'd find her—or she'd find him. And together, they'd figure out a way to conquer level nine.

EMALIA'S LANTERNS
Liana Brooks

LANTERNS LIT THE CITY like nine million stars fallen from the sky. The light reflected off polished marble walls and threw the engraved runes into sharp relief. But at the gates to the under-city, the lanterns ceased. Their light never fell past the dark guardians, jackal-headed beasts carved of star stone who came alive to eat those denizens of the under-city who dared cross into the light.

Down that way, in a warren of mud buildings baked hard by the sun, lived the powerless. The people with no family name, no power, no chance to duel their way to the emperor's throne. Down in the dregs of humanity was where Rion went, jumping over the gates with a push of magic and landing silently on the dusty street.

Here and there, weak candles lit windows covered by tattered cloth. Voices floated through the darkness, fishermen mumbling to themselves as they prepared to hike down to the river Esen as the sun rose in a few hours. Everyone else was asleep. Still, Rion pulled a veil of magic over himself. The scion of the Tahtali house shouldn't be seen here. He shouldn't be anywhere near this part of the desert city, but he could no more stay away than he could breathe underwater.

At last the narrow streets led him to a small plaza with a communal well that reached deep into the mountain. Here was one corner of the lower city that could belong to the city above, one corner where hard mud was carved with flowing glyphs of power. He traced a name he loved better than his own and looked up to her window. "Emalia?"

Lantern light flared purple behind a curtain of silk. A silhouette appeared and then the curtains were drawn aside to reveal the face of his beloved. Dark hair fell around the face of a goddess and every thought save one scattered. Twelve days had passed since he'd last seen her, last felt her touch, heard the whisper of her voice in his mind.

Emalia's thoughts didn't seem headed in the same direction. Her lips twitched into a wry smile he knew from a thousand fights in the dueling rings at the citadel. "Why are you courting death?"

"Because I haven't persuaded you to come live in the city proper yet." A wisp of her magic coiled around him, exciting every nerve in his body. "Let me come up."

There was a laugh as the curtain fell again, and then the sound of stone grinding against stone as she lifted her wards. His heart raced in anticipation. The bastard daughter of a bastard. An outcast with no name. But her magic. Her mind! From the first time she'd spoken in the square in the magi's class, he couldn't look away.

Three years had been wasted trying to tease her family name from her, trying to buy her in the time-honored traditions of his ancestors. One night, in utter despair, he had wandered the dark city, seen her, and followed, intent only on finding her family name. She'd led him here, into the very heart of darkness, and in a breath he'd thrown away everything for her. The emperor's law decreed that no unnamed child with magic should live. Yet Emalia lived, and he didn't have the heart to turn her over.

Two more years had passed while he jealously guarded her secret. Two years of yearning before he confessed everything in the desert under the light of a waning moon. Two years fearing he would lose what he could never call his own. And now twelve days apart felt like the cold fingers of death.

Emalia opened the door to her shop wearing little more than a gauzy tunic that dropped to her knees. Even the insignificant candlelight pierced that thin veil, revealing a body that would tempt any man. "Weren't you supposed to be in the western desert for another fortnight?"

"I was, but I was called back early for a trivial matter. I'll leave again in the morning." He reached for her, needing to hold her, needing to have her with him as desperately as a fish needed the sea.

"A trivial matter? I heard you dueled with Kherei and left him blind. He's not unpowerful."

"He's a foolish boy rushing for the title of magi by challenging those he thinks weaker. His eyes will heal in a month or two and the time away from the citadel will be good for him."

She crossed her arms. "He would kill you if he could. Would you make me a widow before you make me a wife?"

"My love, my steadfast star and only light!" Rion picked her up and swung her around. "Only one magi in this city could ever beat me in dueling arena, and you are she. My perfect rival, Emalia." He kissed her, drinking her in, feeling the pulse of her blood coursing through her, feeling her magic seep through his skin until they were one.

They danced up the stairs, the memories of a thousand nights spent just like this woven into every step. Her tunic dropped beside his armor. The brush of cold air on his skin made him shiver. His hunger fueled her passion. By dawn's light both had forgotten where the individual ended and the lover began.

Emalia rested her head on Rion's shoulder, lazily tracing a scar on his chest. "You are worried."

"There's trouble brewing in the city and I have to patrol the desert and leave you behind."

She laughed. "Who would come down here?"

"Someone who thinks they can gain some power by denouncing you? Someone who thinks they might challenge a magi to win rank? Some fool man who thinks you are unwed and free for the taking." He scowled.

Emalia propped herself up on one arm to look at him. "Let them come. If the emperor charges me with being a false magi I will challenge him to a duel. Let the challengers come, praying to their false gods for titles; I will kill them all. Let the swains come with their poems and flowers; they will never have me while I live."

"See? I could come back to the city in smoking ruins. Then I would be forced to conquer another because I cannot let you live in a fallen city. And from there, what? Once I lay one city at your feet, it may well become a habit!"

"Will you lay worlds at my feet, magi? Will you give me every breathing thing to rule as I please?"

"If you so wished, it would be done." They kissed, saying more with a touch than any words could ever convey. He knew what she wanted, felt every beat of her heart, and did not doubt she could have the world if she so wished. But his morning and evening star desired no more than his love. She never sought power, only knowledge, and so the world was spared from bowing to a goddess, born the bastard of a bastard in the time before time began.

ANSWER THE QUESTION
Amy Laurens

I TILTED MY HEAD back against the pastel green wall of the day spa, relaxing just enough that I could feel every ache and pain in my body. Man, I was looking forward to this massage.

The door handle on one of the client rooms twisted, and a fraction of a second before the door opened, I stiffened. Heat sang through my body and, furious, I stuffed it away. Not Brandr. For a brief moment I panicked, wondering if Bianca had mixed things up and booked my massage with him again—but I forced myself to breathe and relax, keeping my eyes closed. Bianca ran her day spa with a golden heart and an iron fist; she wouldn't do that to me.

Still, as Brandr exited the client room and crossed the waiting area, footsteps soft on the rugged floor, I felt more than heard him pause in front of me, every sense in my body standing to rigid attention.

Steady breath in, steady breath out. Steady breath in, steady breath out. I'd managed to successfully ignore him through all of our infrequent encounters since that first massage, and today would be no different.

In front of me, he sniffed. "I clearly need to have a word with Bianca," he muttered, and I couldn't tell if he was including me in his audience or not. "That lounge needs replacing, and some things around here are getting downright old and worn."

I managed to avoid choking on my disbelief until he left the room, though I could still see the back of his head disappearing down the stairs, so doubtless he heard me. Whatever. I didn't even care. Stupid, arrogant, jerk-faced *twat*. Just because he was so pretty that girls fell over themselves to be near him. Well, I wasn't falling for it, even if it *had* been the best bloody massage of my life. I was not some stupid, vapid piece of arm-candy for him to play with. Urgh.

I slammed my head back against the wall just a little too hard, and winced. *Moron. Imbecile! Arrogant peacocky slimeball!*

"Ellie?" Bianca's soothing voice halted my litany and I sighed, forcing away the negative energy that encounters with Brandr always left me. "Your turn, honey."

Damn him. I was going to enjoy my massage. He was not going to ruin this perfect moment of relaxation. Firmly shoving thoughts of stunningly gorgeous manwhores from mind, I followed Bianca into a treatment room.

• • • ⌇⌇⌇ • • •

I slid into my regular seat at Felici's just as Nana and Tanya, my older sister, were handing their menus to the waitress. "I'll have the usual," I said as the waitress raised an eyebrow at me.

She nodded and swept away, leaving behind a cobalt blue bottle that sparkled and dripped with condensation.

"So," I said, pouring water for everyone, "what's new?"

Tanya shrugged. "Nothing much. Working retail during the holiday season still sucks. Though at least Brandr is on this afternoon, so things won't be deadly boring until he finishes up at six."

The glass I reached for slipped, tipped, and sailed towards the floor. Nana, with characteristic lightning reflexes, caught it before it had barely left the table, setting it upright and relieving me of my water-pouring duties.

"Brandr works at the boutique as well?" I said, aiming for nonchalant.

Nana smirked, and I pointedly ignored her.

Sister nodded. "Oh, yeah. He does mornings in the spa and afternoons downstairs in the storefront."

I made a careful mental note to avoid Schwab in the afternoons. Not that I needed much help with that; Schwab was a designer boutique selling jewellery and cosmetics that were at least four times out of my price range. I'd known they were affiliated with the day spa, but I hadn't realised they shared staff. I guess it made sense, especially for the cosmetics and beauty product sales.

Whatever. Irrelevant. I shoved the whole issue aside and turned to Nana. "So, I was thinking of hitting up the department store this afternoon. I need some clothes for work. Do you want to come?" Not only did Nana have impeccable taste, she also had an almost-bottomless bank account, and she had no qualms about sharing it with her two surviving family members.

She nodded decisively. "Yes," she said. "It will be illuminating."

My eyebrows knitted in puzzlement, but I let it pass. Nana was well known for her bizarre comments and apparently unconnected observations. "Sure," I said. "Thank you."

"Swing by Schwab when you're done," Tanya said. "I'm stuck there till eleven tonight. I'll take my break when you come."

Nana was already agreeing enthusiastically, and I groaned. So much for avoiding the place.

Never mind. We'd go in, find Tanya, and drag her out for a break. The chances of running into Brandr were entirely minimal. Everything would be fine.

"I'll just be a second," I assured Nana as I ducked into the shopping centre bathroom. We'd spend a good couple of hours clothes-hunting, and all of the resulting outfits were nicer than what I had on now. If we were only stopping past Schwab to collect Tanya, my chances of running into Brandr were minimal (thank heavens), but if we did I wasn't interested in providing more fodder for insults. Old and tired. Prat.

Locked safely in a stall, I surveyed my options. The navy was too formal; the silver too attention-seeking. I settled on a neutral-toned skirt that showed off my butt and a red silk blouse with fluttery cap sleeves that managed to actually make me look like I had cleavage. The whole outfit was chic yet effortless, the neutral skirt enriching the light brown of my hair and the red blouse the best possible colour for my skin tone.

I pulled it all on, slipped on some gorgeous new shoes—it was so shallow of me, but I did love Nana's bank account—fluffed my hair, and headed back out.

Nana whistled. "Don't you look special," she said.

I smiled distractedly, running my fingers along the blouse's neckline. "It's missing something," I said. "I need something around my neck."

Nana shrugged. "If you say so."

I loaded my bags back into the trolley and marched off determinedly. Three times Nana tried to draw my attention to jewellery stores we passed, but I knew exactly the one I was after.

We rounded the corner: Schwab. Narrowing my eyes, I made a beeline for the main jewellery display in the back of the store.

Nana caught up after a few moments, and eyed the dazzling array of entirely over-the-top necklaces, the lightest of which looking like it had to weigh at least a pound. "These aren't really what you're looking for, dear," she observed candidly.

I shrugged, stifling irritation. "I thought they'd have a bigger range. This one's okay," I added, pointing out a silver filigreed piece with a floral motif.

Voices erupted around the end of the aisle and I froze. *I will not turn around. I will not turn around.* I realised I was checking myself out in the mirror to make sure the outfit was sitting right, and jerked my gaze away. "Or this one." I reached for another necklace to my left, conveniently allowing me to turn my back on the approaching Prince of Twathood.

Nana, of course, turned towards him. "Oh, *I* see. Of course."

Was it permissible to hit grandmothers for being smug? If it had been Tanya, I'd have whacked her for sure.

"I'll just wait out the front, I think," Nana continued, oblivious to my glares. "My feet, you know. And my hips. And my back." She hobbled away to the tables out the front, looking every day of her age—which I'd never seen her do when she wasn't up to mischief.

I was too busy fuming at her retreating back to realise that Brandr had come within range.

"Can I help you?" he said, eyes dancing.

No. I was *not* looking at his stupid pretty eyeballs. I whirled back to the jewellery display. "That one," I said primly. "I'd like to try it on please."

He reached for the necklace that hung just out of my reach, brushing past my shoulder in the process. I jolted at the energy his touch sent through me and ended up three feet away down the aisle. My stupid reflexes were always a little unpredictable, but they seemed worse when he was around. This had been an utterly ridiculous idea. So what if he thought I looked old and tired? Why did I care what he thought?

"Here."

I turned back to him, expecting to see the silver filigree. Instead, he held a ropey, glimmering creation I could have sworn wasn't on the shelves a moment ago. It was a single necklace, but made up of tens or maybe even hundreds of strands; I couldn't quite get a fix on it to figure it out; the threads seemed unnaturally fine and soft, like spider's silk, the beads tiny and delicate as dewdrops. It glimmered gently in the fluorescent lights of the store, and I stood motionless, transfixed.

"Do you like it?" There was a depth of emotion to Brandr's voice that I'd never heard before, and my heart skipped a beat in response.

"Yes," I breathed, awkwardness and irritation forgotten.

Brandr beamed and my pulse skipped again. Saints, he was beautiful. Too beautiful, like a dangerous snake, but as he moved towards me with the necklace in hand, I was powerless to break the spell.

He reached for me and I turned to face the mirror, my back to him so he could fasten the necklace around my neck. Instead, he laid one end of it across my forehead and directed me to hold it in place while he arranged the rest of the multitude of strands through the back of my hair, half catching it up in a style that seemed at once impossibly complex and incredibly simple.

He fastened the catch on the jewellery just above my left ear and dropped a strand of hair to cover it. I stared at the mirror, lost for words. The necklace—headpiece—whatever it was—had glimmered before, but in my hair it shone. I felt like I was wearing a headdress of moonlight that seemed to pulse gently in time with my breaths.

"Stunning."

I glanced up at Brandr in the mirror, surprised to see his eyes shining wetly. That instant was enough to break the spell though, and I turned. "Let me show Nana," I said. "I mean, let me see what she thinks."

He stepped back, deferential. "Of course."

Out the front of the store I found Tanya engaged in vibrant conversation with Nana, who sat with her back to me. Tanya's eyes widened as she spotted me. She paused mid-sentence. Nana twisted in her chair to see what Tanya had seen—and her hand flew to her mouth.

"Oh," she said as I drew close. "Oh, Elyena. You have it in your hair."

I shrugged, suddenly embarrassed. "Oh, well," I said, tugging on the strands across my forehead. "Brandr thought he'd try something different."

"Brandr did this?" Nana asked. She turned back to her table and busied herself in her copious handbag before I could reply.

Irritated, I snagged the necklace and tugged it down over my face. I shook my hair free from it and twisted it around to hang around my neck. Stupid Brandr and his stupid ideas. What was he playing at, anyway?

"There," I snapped at the table, Tanya already engrossed in a new conversation with Brandr, and Nana still rummaging in her bag. Seriously, would it kill them to focus on me for more than a second? "Now what do we think?" I twitched the luminous white strands that trailed down my chest, still beautiful, but lacking the glorious beauty they'd had in the mirror just before.

He narrowed his eyes critically at me. "The shirt does alluring things to your cleavage, I'll give you that, even if it does emphasise your wide shoulders. I still wish you'd let me trim your hair, your forehead's getting completely lost..." He trailed off under my glare. "No?"

"I *meant* about the *necklace*." My voice was remarkably calm for someone struggling not to commit homicide.

Beside him, Tanya laughed. "I'm sorry. I've been training him for months, and he's still barely housebroken." She turned to him. "Brandr, what's our mantra? Answer the question..."

"Nothing else." He nodded. "Answer the question, nothing else."

They repeated it again together before dissolving into giggles.

I shook my head. "I'll just, uh, go put this back then, shall I?"

"Yes, dear," Nana said. "You can try to do that if you like."

I rolled my eyes at her theatrics and headed for the back of the store. I hunted the display shelf for a place to hang the necklace. Oddly, there didn't seem to be any empty hooks. I ran the necklace through my fingers, glancing down at where it hung limply around my neck. It was pretty—magically so—but it lacked the sparkle, the mysterious something else I'd thought it had when Brandr had first put it on me.

On a whim, I faced the mirror and tugged the necklace back up into my hair, trying to mimic the style Brandr had created. Soft strands fell over my forehead and caught my hair partially up; it wasn't quite how he'd done it, but... I tilted my head at the mirror and my heart skipped a beat.

Hesitantly, I reached up to touch the gossamer strands where they glimmered and glowed like a slipped halo.

Something solid hit me across the backs of my thighs. I flailed wildly for balance and found myself clinging to Brandr's head, as he pranced wildly around the store with me on his shoulders, shouting, "Answer the question, nothing more! Answer the question, nothing more!"

Oh saints, my stomach's showing. I tugged awkwardly at my shirt, caught between momentary embarrassment and his wildly infectious enthusiasm. "But what's the question?" I shouted over the din, too disoriented by suddenly being on his shoulders to think of anything better to say.

He laughed. "The necklace! It works!"

"Um, yay?"

Brandr performed some complicated sort of movement that removed me from his shoulders and ended up with me in his arms. "Yay?" he said, eyes oddly serious in contrast to the frivolity of the situation.

"Well," I said, waving my hands as vaguely as I felt, "It works, right? So yay?" I still had no idea what 'working' entailed, but whatever it was, apparently this was Christmas for Brandr. He hugged me tightly to him and where our skin touched fire rippled through me. Saints. I'd forgotten what it felt like to have actual proper skin contact with him, not just accidental brushes I did my best to avoid.

It was like drowning, and it was addictive, and it was probably just my imagination that my necklace halo was glowing like it might go nova and Brandr was holding me, touching me, and my hands were wrapping around the back of his neck and through his hair as the air around us burst with perfect, glorious pleasure. Skin. I needed his skin.

My stomach flipped as something happened to gravity and I had a brief impression of broken plasterboard and a flash of darkness before Brandr lay me down somewhere soft, and all I cared about was the touch of his skin, because it was beautiful, and perfect, and I nearly sobbed as heat soaked through me, lighting up every fibre of my being and chasing out fear and doubt and darkness—except just *there*, in my head, the seat of logic and rationality. *It* remained unmoved, a cold stone trying to catch my attention in the wave of heat.

"Wait," I gasped. I needed a moment to process this.

He ignored me, hands rubbing at my shoulders just like they had that first time in—

I took in the plush-rugged floor, the pastel green walls, the ivory couches around the perimeter of the room. We were in the day spa. I struggled semi-upright. "Wait! How on earth did we..."

He paused, and I found the gaping hole in the floor. Vague memories of a surge of power, of Brandr springing upwards ten metres or more to the roof—*through* the roof—through the *floor*... I stared at him, wide-eyed, the magma flow of heat suddenly halted. "What are you?"

"Happy," he mumbled against my shoulder.

I whacked him gently on the back of the neck. "Answer the question," I said.

"Nothing more," he murmured, nuzzling my neck. My skin fizzed where his lips touched, and I had to concentrate to rap him on the back of the head.

"Yes," I said. "Nothing more."

He sat back, eyes clouded with lust slowly clearing. "I am what you are, Love: a child of the gods. Well, I am closer than you: my mother was a goddess. Your grandmother is the actual godling in your family."

My heart stalled. Child of the gods? Me? *Nana?*

Actually, I had to admit that made a hell of a lot of sense. Nana's bizarre observations, her uncanny sense of timing, her ridiculous physical abilities... I blinked, unsure what was more unsettling: that my grandmother was a godling, or that it was dead easy to believe it.

"Hold on, wait," I said, wriggling further out from underneath Brandr. "If you're a godling, then..." I hesitated, not sure how to phrase my question, and not sure I wanted to know the answer. A godling. No wonder girls of all ages threw themselves at him. How many women had he loved in his lifetime? Ten? Twenty? A hundred?

Cold logic was almost as good as a cold shower. "No," I said. "No."

"No what?"

"No-I-am-*not*-going-to-be-the-latest-in-a-long-line-of-floozies no. Not interested. I don't care what you are, I'm not available."

His eyes widened, body and face alike drooping in disappointment. "But Love, you feel it, I know you do."

"Feel what?" I snapped, arms wrapped tightly around my torso. I felt nothing that he didn't manipulate me to feel with his stupid godly powers.

"This," he whispered, and reached out. His fingertip connected softly with the corner of my jaw, and I swallowed against the melting heat that tried to consume me. His finger trailed down my neck, tracing a blissful line across the hollow of my clavicle, lighting fire oh-so-carefully down my sternum.

He pulled away and I remembered how to breathe.

"See?" he said, still whispering. "How can you deny it?"

I shook my head, tears burning my eyes. *I don't want this, I don't want this,* I reminded myself frantically. "It isn't real." My nails dug into my palms as I stared into his sea-green eyes, so full of sadness they seemed a mirror of my own.

"Tell me..." I drew in a shaky breath. "Answer the question."

He nodded, gaze searching my face like an enigma.

"How many other girls?"

Brandr frowned, and sadness turned to confusion.

I rolled my eyes, flicking away tears with a quick finger. "Don't give me that. How many other girls have you played this game with, made... feel like this?" I wasn't holding my breath for his answer. I wasn't.

His confusion deepened. "But Love, I couldn't."

It was my turn to be confused. "What do you mean?"

He shook his head. "I couldn't *make* someone feel like this. When I touch you, I feel what you feel. I felt it that first time, do you remember? The massage?"

Saints, how I had tried to forget. His touches had been perfectly innocent, utterly professional, but the fire they'd awoken in me had left me reeling in terror; I'd never felt anything so strong in my life.

A tiny smile played at the corners of his mouth. "That's when I knew."

My heart pounded in my head, my chest—and everywhere else. "Knew what?"

He was leaning closer, lips a mere breath away, and I didn't want to be a conquest, but now that I thought about it—really and truly thought about it, without the filter of frustration and jealousy—could it be? Was I really the only girl actually losing her head over this man, the only one struggling not to throw herself at his feet?

"I knew," he whispered against my ear, and I almost couldn't hear him through the ecstasy echoing through my body, "that you were the one."

"I don't believe in soulmates," I whispered back, eyes closed, every sense in my body standing to attention as his cheek tickled against mine.

"You don't have to." His lips traced my jaw and I shivered. "Your heart recognises me, Love, whether you believe in it or not."

"Love," I whispered, fingers tightening in his hair. "Is that what this is?"

"It could be," he said. "If you wanted it to be."

I luxuriated in the thought for just a moment, before another one hit me. I bolted upright, narrowly avoiding a collision with his nose. "Wait just one second here, buddy. Old? You think I look tired and old?" His words from that morning rang in my ear. "Not to mention, oh, I don't know, my too-broad shoulders and my totally-lost forehead!" I glared at him, wishing that godling powers included the ability to set someone literally on fire.

Brandr laughed, a soft, throaty chuckle that sounded far too appealing. "I knew you'd take it like that, and I confess, I half hoped I'd provoke you into responding. But if you recall, I said that *some* things around here were getting downright old and worn. I mean, Love, your constant indifference. Not *you*."

He tracked a finger over my hairline, leaving tingling fireworks in its wake.

"That's nice," I said, pushing his hand away, "But what about my shoulders? And my forehead?"

He frowned, confusion plain again. "What about them?"

"You..." I squirmed, uncertain how to voice my fears aloud without sounding insecure and needy. "They're not 'too broad', and, well, you know...?"

"Look at me, Love," he said. "Am I perfect?"

YES, my heart screamed. YES YOU ARE BLOODY PERFECT. But I shoved the scrambling emotions away and forced myself to look. Cold logic; cold shower; I could do this. And true, now he mentioned it, his nose leaned a bit to one side, and one eye was slightly larger than the other, and if I was going to be utterly picky then his forehead was probably a fraction too large, and... "Oh."

Brandr softened into a smile. "Answer the question, Love."

"Yes," I said. "And no. I see what you mean. You mean that—"

He pressed a finger against my lips. "Answer the question, Love, but nothing more." His eyes sparkled.

I smiled.

He leaned down and kissed me, and this time, I kissed him back.

NOT QUITE CINDERELLA
Liana Brooks

"HAVE YOU HEARD? THE prince is giving a ball!"

"In the middle of a war?" Marian looked at the thin, sallow, pastry chef behind the counter who didn't look like he'd ever tasted his own wares. "Are you serious? A party during a major offensive?"

The sallow chef nodded eagerly. "Oh, yes! The prince will choose a bride, the king will abdicate, and the whole war will be over."

Marian nodded slowly, weighing the options. "So, what I'm hearing is, your side is losing?"

"My side?" The thin man looked confused.

"The king is losing, isn't he?"

The man's eyes widened. "I would never suggest something so traitorous!"

"Of course not." She gave him a polite smile. "A fudge brownie please." She pointed to the rich confection and waited as he bagged her purchase. Her sponsors couldn't afford for the war to end now.

"Three coppers."

She slid a silver piece across the counter. "The stars shine on those who show charity today," she said and walked out with the brownie, skirts swirling around her. An end to the war. Not good. Still, it could be fixed easily enough. Plans began to circulate through her mind.

The baker wasn't the only one with the news of the ball. In the centre of town the square buzzed with people rushing to prepare for the upcoming party. Dress shops, barely open for the day, had lines of customers and coaches waiting outside. The grocer's cart was empty. Flower sellers were scarce, or possibly just waiting in line for a seasonable dress.

One very determined hat seller stepped into Marian's path, advancing at her with a bright green horror stuffed with purple feathers. "Have you something fetching to wear to the ball, Mi'lady?"

"No," Marian said, trying to sidestep the feather tickling her nose.

"Have you considered green, Mi'lady? It would be a most becoming color on you."

"Yes, if I had darker skin or fairer hair I'm sure it would. But since I have neither, I think perhaps not." She offered the hat seller a strained smile.

"Purple?" The hat seller waved the plumes closer to her face.

"No, lime and plum aren't the right shades for me," she said. *Or anyone with a modicum of taste.* "Thank you."

The hat seller pounced, placing the hat on her head and stabbing it in place with a five-inch hairpin.

Marian glared as she counted, in Greek, to ten. "Remove the hat."

"But for just a few silvers..." the seller wheedled.

"*REMOVE THE HAT.*" Thunder cracked through the clear sky.

The seller grabbed the hat, ripping the felt, and ran.

Marian removed the pin from her hair and tossed it on the ground. Around her, the natives edged away, fearful of what she might do next. She rolled her eyes and walked back to the inn she'd checked into late last night. It wasn't the fanciest place she'd ever spent the night, but it certainly wasn't the worst.

She tossed a small bag of silver pieces to the innkeeper for a hot bath and a warm meal and walked up the stairs, musing over the worst place she'd spent the night. Probably in the burnt-out hovel last year, where the ruins were still smoking and the air smelt of burnt flesh. She'd slept on the floor in the stone cellar, waiting for the pain to stop.

Opening the door to her small room, Marian paused. No, the cellar was the second worst. The first worst had to have been that palace three years back, with the hideous pink silk and white lace covering everything. That was the worst. Definitely.

Someone appeared behind her. "Water, Miss, for your bath, Miss."

She turned and smiled at the fresh-faced maid carrying two buckets of steaming water. "Please, bring them in."

"Here you go, miss. Getting ready for the ball, are you?"

"Me?" Marian shook her head. "I wasn't planning to."

The girl sighed, starry eyed. "Oh, but a ball. Doesn't everyone want to go and dance the night away?"

Marian wrinkled her nose. "Pinched shoes, creaking corsets, and the smell of old women marinating in their perfume? It really isn't that grand."

"But to meet the prince!" The girl put the buckets by the fireplace, not spilling a drop. "I'd love to go, just for that." She didn't swoon, but she did sigh.

Meet the prince, yes. "And I suppose your wicked stepmother is making you stay home and polish the silver?"

The girl blushed. "No, Mother wouldn't mind if I went. But I've nothing to wear. Nothing nice. I wouldn't get past the guards."

Marian debated for a moment, and decided she was feeling generous. She waved her hand. "Nonsense! You're quite a lovely girl. Hurry and draw my bath and perhaps I can find a suitable tip for you."

The girl curtsied. "That's quite all right, Miss. Even if we had a spare silver or two, all the nice dresses have been bought up by now."

Marian shooed her out. "Get my bath and let me worry about the tip." She opened the door to the room's armoire and studied the dresses inside. Fine blonde hair, pink cheeks, deep blue eyes and brown, muddy feet... The girl needed something full length, soft and dusky. Marian discarded red immediately: too wanton. And pink was abjectly cruel: the poor girl would look like a shepherdess who'd lost her nursery rhyme. Blue was the obvious answer, but was it too obvious? Yes, yes it was. She could do better.

From the back of the armoire, she pulled out a lilac gown of silk, with seed pearls and diamonds fastened around the low collar. Perfect. Even if the girl didn't net the prince in this affair (which might be a blessing considering the political situation), she'd find some suitor willing to marry her for the dress alone.

The maid backed into the room, carrying the wooden sitting tub, red and shiny in the face.

"Just set it down there by the fireplace," Marian instructed. "I know it's too warm for a fire, but it does seem the proper place for a bath. Do you have a screen, perchance?" She waved at the view. "The windows are lovely but, well, a maiden and her modesty and all that..."

The maid turned around, nodding again, and stopped to stare at the gown. "Oh! That's the most beautiful thing I've ever seen! Did you change your mind? Are you going tonight after all?"

"Hmm. I may. But this old thing?" Marian made a show of regarding the gown with great skepticism. "It really isn't my color. Far too regal, and too pale for my skin, I think. Do you like it?"

The maid wiped her hands on her own brown skirt before gently running the hem of the lilac gown through her fingers. "It's lovely."

"I really do think it's a tattered old thing. You can have it if you like." Marian tossed the dress at her. "Go and try it on. If you hurry, your mother will have time to fit it to you before the ball."

Her eyes went wide. "But, your bath..."

Marian shrugged. "I can handle that. Go on, have fun tonight." The maid left hurriedly. Marian hummed to herself. She bathed, ate a leisurely meal while watching people bustle through the streets in preparation for the festival, and then took a nap.

She woke when the bell tower tolled ten. With practiced moves, she dressed in a pristine white gown with a belled skirt and a low neckline. A white opal pendant that flashed fire in the candlelight completed the ensemble. In the window she could see her reflection, a perfect vision of a mysterious princess arriving late for the ball. Down in the alley she could even see the perfect coach, just waiting to whisk her away.

How banal.

Marian swept down the stairs and out the back door, unnoticed by the snoozing innkeeper. The coachman didn't say a word as she touched her necklace and tucked her head like a coy ingénue. She smiled to herself as they clattered through the cobblestone streets. Charms were almost cheating. Well, not charms plural, Marian reminded herself; charm, singular, and not the kind that witches and sorceresses used. A single, simple charm to make everyone love her.

There was a momentary twinge of guilt. What if the nice little maid had charmed the prince naturally? Marian furrowed her brow, wondering how she would work that one out. As the coach rolled to a stop at the palace gates and the page ran to open the door, the tower bells chimed eleven. With a sigh, Marian gave up the dilemma. All she could do was hope for the best, and kill anyone who got in her way.

With infinite grace, she swept up the stairs and through the halls, pausing to time her entrance with the final flourish in the music for maximum drama.

The prince's hand dropped away from the waist of the blue-clad beauty he'd been dancing with. Marian curtsied at a distance, hiding a snicker. A pale blue dress on a blue-eyed blonde, with upswept hair? Really? How clichéd could a fairy godmother get? If she had a copper for every time a well-meaning interloper put a blue dress on a blue-eyed girl, she'd have enough for a retirement fund, or at least a vacation somewhere tropical.

She forced a blush as the prince practically ran up the short staircase to bow low over her hand. "May I have this dance?"

"I'd be delighted," she simpered. It took practice to simper, and it paid off. The prince danced her around the room, staring deeply into her eyes like a fool in love.

Later, he took her into the moonlit gardens. "Am I really in love? Or is this some magic? A dream?" he whispered as he leaned close.

"Magic," Marian whispered too. "Charm enchantment."

"Do you love me?" The prince tenderly brushed a finger along her cheek. "I love you."

"I know." She stepped away from him. "But it won't last past dawn."

He stepped closer. "If we have only to dawn, let us dance the night away."

"Virgin!" She smothered a laugh in her hand, pretending to cough. Recovering herself, she smiled at the prince. "I have a carriage. Let's run away together."

He put his hands on her hips and pulled her close. "I'll do anything you say."

"Smart kid." Marian patted his cheek. "Take my hand and lead me the back way to the carriages. And then pick the fastest one."

"Where are we going?" he asked, showing the first real sign of independent thought. A strong-willed person would fight the charm enchantment; the prince wasn't fighting at all. Really, she was doing the kingdom a favor by removing him from the line for the throne. "My love?"

"We're running away together," Marian told him as he led her through dark rose gardens and down marble steps to the courtyard full of carriages. The rub of her knife sheath as she descended the stairs was a comforting caress. "By the way, you have a beautiful castle."

"We have a beautiful castle," he told her. "Forever we, you and I together in love."

"At least until death or dawn do us part." Marian let him hand her into the carriage. In a high up window she saw a young woman, radiant in lilac and diamonds, flirting with a powerful young duke. At least someone would have a happy ending.

AS LONG AS I LIVE
Amy Laurens

I DIDN'T *MEAN* TO abduct the king. Honest I didn't. I'd meant to be good, meant to keep my oath of fealty to him as long as he still drew breath. It wasn't *my* fault he'd chosen that day to be out in a paddock full of cows.

I'd snatched up the first thing I'd been able to reach, assuming it was one of nearly a hundred practically identical black beefers. Honestly, I think I was more surprised than the king was.

"How dare you!" the king blustered as I set him gently on the ground outside my lair. "What did I tell you? If you so much as *touch* another human being, I'll have you slaughtered for meat and magic!"

I ducked my head, embarrassed. "I really am sorry, your Majesty. I was aiming for the cows."

"I don't care what you were aiming for! You picked up *me!*" He straightened his tunic and glared. "I'll not kill you yet, but you will pay for this." He turned on his heel and marched away, but over his shoulder something sleek and dark and dangerous fluttered.

I shrank back, but the glittering darkness homed in. It wound me in silken folds; I shrieked as my wings shredded.

The darkness lifted. The king threw one last look over his shoulder. "You'll never fly to search for prey as long as I live, dragon. It's over. Curl up and die."

Usually, I would have done. For a dragon, I've been pretty obedient, ever since the king took my egg from my mother and left me in my cave. But this was death by slow starvation. I wasn't *that* obedient. Especially if the curse only held as long as he lived.

I pounced. He tasted pretty good, even if my wings did itch a bit as they healed.

OATH BREAKER
Amy Laurens

THE METALLIC SCENT OF blood reached him through the sharpness of the snow. For a moment, his heart leapt and he thought the battle was still raging, the cries of dying men filling his ears and stopping his senses; but no. The mountains up ahead were the foothills of home, and there were no people around, no sounds, no battle cries.

Easing his shoulders under heavy mail—he hadn't dared leave it behind, old Tom would curse him halfway to the grave if he returned without it—he trudged on.

The path crested and he spotted the source of the blood-scent easily: a great dragon, rear half skinned, muscle and sinew left exposed to the elements. Blood had seeped into the snow around it, tinting it pink.

He ran a hand over his face. He'd been at battle for nine and a half months. The war was supposed be over; coming home was supposed to be the end of all the carnage. But no, someone had to drop a stinking great dead dragon in his path. He gritted his teeth, hefted his pack, and trudged towards the beast.

Halfway there the bushes off the side of the path rustled. He barely had time to check that his sword was still in its scabbard before five scruffy-looking bandits appeared, three bearing equally scruffy swords covered in nicks and dings. The other two held rough-hewn bats, and one tried for menacing as he tapped his bat against his free palm.

The soldier sighed and eased his sword free. He could take the five of them on with his eyes closed—but probably not if he tried to keep them all alive. Gods, he was so *tired* of death.

The leader of the bandits swaggered forward. "Come t' steal our dragon, have ye?"

"Put your sword down, mate. All I want to do is go home." The soldier shifted his grip on his own sword in case the bandit lunged.

In response, the bandit sneered. "That's what they all say." He turned to his lackeys. "All right, boys. You know what to do."

He gave them the nod and as one they advanced towards the soldier.

"Please," he said, holding his sword up loosely in one hand. "I won't fight you. I won't fight any longer. Somewhere the fighting must stop. Please, let it be here, now."

The bandits laughed.

"Easy pickings, this one," one of the men said.

"Surprised he came back from the war alive," mused another.

The soldier bowed his head. "So be it," he said. "I vowed not to take a life outside of war, and I will not break that now." He held the sword out in front of him, one hand balancing the grip, the other lightly cupping the flat of the blade. *Gods preserve us all.*

Magic crackled around him. *You do well, vow-keeper. You are worthy.*

A creaky rumble sounded, and before anyone could react, the great dragon's tail swept right through the midst of the bandits, knocking them all off their feet.

Three were immediately rendered unconscious, and without hesitation the solider leapt forward to follow up on his advantage, knocking out a fourth with the flat of his blade. If the only way to avoid death today was to leave them sleeping on the ground, well, his vows had prohibited murder, not violence.

The soldier pivoted as the leader of the bandits cried out and lunged at his shoulder, but the soldier ducked and let the stroke go past. He dodged left, dropped to one knee and drove upwards with the pommel of his sword, aiming for the bandit leader's chin. A nice, steady uppercut ought to do it.

The dragon's claws caught him around the leg, destabilised him. His arms windmilled. The sword twisted point up. The bandit completed his lunge, the sword driving deep into the his throat. Arterial blood spurted, red and bright, life gushing from the man before his eyes.

War cries sounded in his ears, the smell of blood blocked out thought, and the pounding of a thousand warrior feet shook the ground. *No. No, I promised!*

The soldier barely felt it as the dragon shifted its grip and dragged him closer. The smell of rotting meat on the great carnivore's breath mingled with blood until it could have belonged to week-old bodies decaying on the fields, and the pain that lanced through him as the dragon bit down was the piercing of swords. He stared glassy-eyed at the sky as death descended.

A moment passed in rippling pain, and the soldier realised he was on his feet, facing the great dragon while blood dribbled from his shoulder. He clamped down on the wound, noted that the dragon's skin now covered nearly three-quarters of its body, and gazed up at the great iridescent eye.

The dragon turned its head, staring pointedly to where the bandit leader lay dead in a pool of his own blood.

Guilt stung the soldier's chest, and he gulped down air like a man drowning.

Gently, the dragon nudged him with a nose whose nostrils wafted smoke, and the soldier fell down beside the bandit.

"What?" he shouted. "What do you want from me? If you'd just stayed out of it I could have knocked him out! You, you made me kill him. This is your fault!"

But the dragon simply stared, waiting.

Tears streaming down his cheeks, the soldier gathered up the bandit in his arms. Yes, the bandit had initiated the attack, and yes, it couldn't be doubted that the corpse in front of him had belonged to a bad man. But his vows. To lose them over such a senseless death.

He'd had enough of senselessness. He pressed his forehead to the bandit's. "I'm sorry," he whispered. "I didn't mean for you to die."

The bandit stirred in his lap, head tossing, eyes twitched beneath closed lids. The wound in his neck ceased bleeding; the skin began infinitesimally to seal.

The soldier's gaze flicked to his own shoulder, where the bite mark had nearly closed beneath the tear in his chain-mailed shirt, then to the dragon, who was now fully clothed in skin again but for its tail.

You would have sacrificed yourself to preserve your oath. Now you may keep it forever. The dragon stretched like a cat waking from a nap, extended its wings with a single mighty flap, and leapt into the sky.

"Thank you," the soldier murmured, eyes wide. "Thank you."

MY GRANDMOTHER CARRIES A MACHETE
Liana Brooks

MY GRANDMOTHER CARRIES A machete.

Really, it isn't anything cool or exciting. She doesn't fight crime or monsters. It's just a gardening tool. And once you see the garden you realize what she really needs is napalm.

The garden of terror that requires a machete to hack your way to the center started life as a discreet herb garden on the side of the house. It's older than my grandmother, planted by some pioneering ancestor with more enthusiasm than gardening skill.

Planted by someone who didn't realize that those small plants in tidy rows would grow so that the rosemary now resembles a short tree and the parsley is dense enough that small tribes of toddlers have been lost in there.

Perhaps the planter thought the Texas heat would be enough to keep the garden from taking on a life of its own.

Certainly it's a theory that works for the rest of Texas. The easiest way to kill a plant is leave it outside during the month of August and wait for the plant to shoot itself in despair. Even cacti wither and die under the unrelenting heat of the Texas sun.

But not in grandma's garden.

You can ignore the garden, walk away for months at a time, leave it unwatered for years, drop weed killer on it, curse it, exorcise it, even burn incense over it—and yet the garden grows.

My great-grandmother tried giving the plants away. She uprooted the mint and gave it away to everyone who made eye contact. During the worst of Texas droughts you can tell who has the monster mint.

The media dubbed it the "Glenwood Mint". The scientists at Texas A&M are still studying rogue clippings, trying to determine how a plant can live with four-inch roots and no water for two years.

That's why Grandma needs the machete.

Every spring, around about March, she pulls the polished weapon from the cupboard over the washing machine, dons her gardening gloves and sandals, and marches into the backyard to see what damage has been done.

This year is different.

She sits in her rocking chair on March second, a tear in her eye as she watches the snapdragons bloom along the front walk. "I can't do it this year," she whispers. She raises a papery hand, sets it on my knee. "Jenny. Go get the machete. It's your turn."

This is it. With a sense of impending doom, I walk into the mudroom. I pull on the gloves and the sandals. I pull the machete from its case, put my cell phone in my pocket in case I need to call for back up, march into the living room and out the back door.

"Grandma! There are tomatoes!"

Grandma moves with blazing speed to peer over my shoulder. "Good googlymoogly," she breathes. "I forgot about them."

"We haven't planted tomatoes in two years!" I choke back fear. Four lush plants beckon, their red fruit tempting the sinner like apples of Eden.

"Get the pots!"

There are four burners on the stove, each large enough to hold a twenty-two gallon stockpot. We have two slow cookers, and each can hold sixteen gallons. I plunder the tomato orchard. The abandoned plants have grown well over six feet tall; they droop with heavy fruit and spring upright as I pull the tomatoes away.

Stuffing the tomatoes into pots and piling the excess on the long kitchen counter, my grandmother pours water over each set and turns on the heat. "Get garlic," she orders. "You'll find it behind the roses."

I shudder, grab the machete, and stalk into the herb garden of terror.

The rosemary bush towers over me, a fragrant giant. Thick stalks of parsley reach to my knees. But all I can smell is the mint.

In the far corner, I see the rambling roses that cascade over the front fence in a shower of red and pale pink. Beneath those roses, the fresh garlic grows. I heft the machete in my hand. With grim determination I set out, hacking, slashing, pruning with fervor that is nigh on religious.

I bring the slaughter to Grandma: rosemary twigs as long as my arm, bunches of parsley, enough oregano to stuff a piñata, garlic, wild onions that I found tucked in a corner next to the lavender.

"Tell your cousins to bring garlic bread," Grandma instructs as she stirs the six pots, tasting, testing, and adjusting the flavors until they are perfect. "And call the in-laws, we need extra noodles!"

I go back to the garden to trim yellowed leaves that have never seen sunlight. I slip on fresh loam; my cell phone flies. I scream as my cell phone slips between the thorny canes of the roses, another casualty of the garden of terror. But from my prone position I see a miracle: basil!

"Grandma! Basil!" I hold the aromatic leaves up for her distant perusal.

"The mint must have insulated them from the snow this winter."

I labor my way back to her, bearing my bounty. She rubs the leaves between her fingers, releasing the scent like a lover's perfume. "Perfect."

⌁⌁⌁

The next day, as rosy-fingered dawn reaches out to her fleeing love, I roll out of bed and reach for the machete. My machete. I have a cell phone to save and a legacy to keep. The garden must be tamed.

"Holler if you find a body!" Grandma calls.

I walk out the door.

I carry a machete.

VENUS
Liana Brooks

VENUS WALKED THROUGH THE main door as thunder rolled overhead and the rain began to fall. She glared over her shoulder at the rain, then flounced to the front desk of the most expensive hotel in New York City. "Reservation for Vanessa Rome please." She gave the concierge her best smile. He didn't look dazzled.

He tilted his balding head forward to peer at the computer screen. "I'm sorry, ma'am, we don't have a reservation for anyone by that name."

Venus sighed. "My Daddy made the reservation for me, can you check for Dios Rome, please?" Again she smiled dazzlingly at him.

"I'm sorry, ma'am, but the only reservation we have for that name was last month. My computer shows that no one claimed the room and the card used to reserve it was charged for the full three days. Are you certain you didn't get your travel dates wrong?"

She did a quick mental count. "Blast, what's his name changed the calendars, didn't he?"

"Ma'am?"

"The one with the green shorts," Venus raged, godly powers overflowing. She wiped away a tear of frustration from her eye. "Daddy never remembers the date changes. The two extra months and the New Year starting in the middle of winter rather than when Persephone returns from Hades. It's really too much!"

"Of course." The concierge cleared his throat. "Would you like me to call you a cab, ma'am?"

"A cab?"

"Yes, a cab, we're fully booked this evening. I can't offer you a new reservation."

"You can't?"

"No, ma'am. We're full. You will need to go somewhere else."

Venus's immortal power surged, her eyes narrowed, and she balled her fists, ready to attack her victim.

"Gregory?" A blonde woman pushed past her, rushing to the concierge.

"Marian?" He stared at her in shock. "I haven't seen you.... I meant to.... I can explain..."

"Oh, Gregory, there's nothing to explain! I understand perfectly and my answer is"—she blushed and looked down—"yes. Yes, I will marry you!"

As the happily reunited couple burst into a frenzy of sweet coos, whispered promises, and lusty kisses, Venus altered the guest book. A few minor changes and the penthouse-with-a-view was hers.

She cleared her throat. "My reservation," she reminded the lipstick-covered man. "I'd like my room key, thank you. Now."

"Yes, of course, right away." He didn't even question how his full hotel suddenly had a penthouse free.

Venus took the room key with a final look of disgust.

"The room will be ready in an hour." The woman trying to give him mouth-to-mouth resuscitation swallowed up the man's line of patter.

"Jupiter almighty!" Venus swung her multi-colored Fendi handbag and stalked back out into the night. The thunder grumbled overhead as the rain subsided. Her gold Gucci heels clicked on the cement as she tried to breath the fetid city air.

A Mercedes drove past, splashing her shimmering dress with water. Her fists clenched. "How dare you!" With a graceful flick of her wrist, Venus dried her dress. She tossed her perfect mane of golden hair and crossed with the light.

Immortal wrath churned, reaching out to punish the horrible human. A horn blared, tires squealed, and the crunch of a black Mercedes hitting a mini-van sounded. Venus looked back with an evil smile.

The woman in the Mercedes jumped out, nearly tripping over a manhole, raging at the driver of the mini-van. He got out, yelled at her, yelled again in delight when he realized who he was yelling at, and they started kissing.

"Jupiter almighty, you've got to be kidding me!" Venus moaned as the on-lookers clapped. A media-outlets man-on-the-street cam stopped to interview the happily reunited couple. "It's so unfair!"

She kept walking, window shopping through the best part of the city, while all around her, smited humans fell in love, rekindled old romances, decided to give love a chance. Her stomach roiled as a feuding couple in a café put differences aside so they could kiss and make-up. Despondent, Venus slunk into a shabby bookstore and curled up in an over-stuffed armchair to sip a hot cocoa with extra whipped cream.

"Bad day?" the barista asked as she placed a napkin next to Venus on the side table.

"The worst! My reservations at the hotel were messed up, I just had a fight with my husband, and now everywhere I look people are falling in love again. I hate that!"

"Too bad," the girl says without sympathy.

"What about you?" Venus asked with a sniffle. "You have some hot body to curl up with tonight?"

"Nope. I prefer cold and dead." The girl slipped her a card before walking away: *Hit Girls: Taking care of problems and cleaning your closet since 1982. First time free.*

Venus turned the card over, thinking. It wasn't that she didn't love Vulcan. It was more that he didn't understand why she was always with Mars. After all, it was blazingly obvious to everyone but her jealous husband why she was with him. Mars was a wonderful shopping buddy; he understood why she needed more sling-back pumps, he could match colors, and he was madly in love with his hair-stylist from Tulsa. Vulcan just didn't understand.

With a snap of her fingers the card vanished. Hit girls, hit men, hit whatever... That wasn't what she needed.

"David?" The barista was staring at her new customer as if he'd grown a third head.

The Hollywood hero smiled as he pulled a gun. "Sorry, Babes, you know how it is."

"But, we, I ..." A coffee mug dropped from her hands, shattering on the ground as the barista backed away.

The man stood.

The ground shook.

The door to the bookstore opened. Lightning cut across the sky, silhouetting a familiar form. He walked in, adjusting glasses that hid his too-green eyes. The well-cut suit he wore accented his well-muscled frame.

Venus sighed. The Romans had it all wrong. She'd definitely married the hottest man on Olympus Mons.

Vulcan sat down across from her. "I'm sorry."

She sat up. Vulcan never said sorry. In their long, tempestuous marriage, she could count the number of apologies he'd given on one hand. He never *said* sorry, but he showed it in the little things he did. A new vase of black glass, diamonds, a new mountain range in some far-off tropical locale...

"Come on, don't make me say it again."

Venus shook her head and put her mug down with care. "No. You're sorry? Really?"

"I went to surprise you with Mars..." He broke off and blushed.

Venus blushed in sympathy. Vulcan wasn't just near-sighted, sometimes he was downright blind. She cleared her throat. "He's a nice boy, and they make each other happy."

Vulcan turned bright red. "It's just, I expected... Jupiter!" He leaned towards her. "Venus, you're so beautiful I can't imagine how any man would turn you away for, for... anyone else."

Venus studied her nails with interest. There was a story there. If you got upset because the boy you love swung the other way, well, blame it on Hera. Venus knew and was keeping the blackmail tucked away for a rainy day.

"Don't worry about. I never notice them. Just you." She smiled up at Vulcan, batted her eyelashes, took his breath away...

Behind them the world began to move again. David stepped forward, gun still aimed at the betrayed barista's heart. The coffee-girl tilted her chin up defiantly. "Go ahead, you've already broken my heart."

Vulcan looked over and then winked at Venus. "Aren't you going to give the girl a break?"

Venus smiled.

David dropped the gun. "Marry me. We'll run away together. No one ever needs to know..."

SEVEN REASONS I SAID NO: A LIST BY KELLY ANN MORGANSTEIN

Liana Brooks

1.   *It was Nathaniel.*
2.   *He stumbled the proposal and my father finished for him.*
3.   *Instead of a nice dinner out and a ring, my mother made him dinner at our house and he asked during the salad course. No ring.*
4.   *Nathaniel wears yellow socks.*
5.   *I'm pretty sure he snores.*
6.   *Mallory would murder me if I said yes.*
7.   *Nathaniel is dead.*

I MEAN, SERIOUSLY??? A zombie? How's a nice Jewish girl *supposed* to respond? Sure, I'm his last hope for a nice relationship because every other girl has either turned him down or waived a crucifix at him. I get that. Really. But did he need to *tell* me I was his last choice?

So, you know, not only would he not ask me out if I were the last girl on the planet, he literally wouldn't ask me out unless I was the last girl on the planet who hadn't said no *and* he was dead.

That's just cruel.

And having my parents there? Is it too much to ask for a real proposal? You know, a romantic moonlit walk on the beach... Or a day at the museum, followed by a luscious dinner. Something impressive. Sweet potato latkes are tasty, but they aren't romantic. Not when you help make them and have to wash the dishes afterward. And not when the best compliment of the evening is a dead guy telling you you're very obedient.

Obedient? Gosh, Nathaniel! That's just what every girl wants to hear!

You know. When they're three >.<

Not when they're twenty-four and the only single girl in the whole freakin' town. Single, and living in my parent's attic. Anne Frank never had it this bad. Right now, I'd welcome a world war.

Anything to keep nosey Mrs. S from dropping by tomorrow for breakfast when she will, I guarantee, casually grab my hand, intending to inspect the rock. Boy is *she* in for a surprise.

You know what I have instead of a ring? A bracelet. One of Nathaniel's. From the hospital. And his original toe tag. So I could be near him or something? I have no clue. It was creepy. I wanted to set fire to him but my mom grabbed the candles before I could.

Back-stabbing mother! Does she really want a half-rotted corpse as a son-in-law? Is she actually that desperate?

I've got to move out. It's the only logical choice. I need to go find my own place and find someone else to date. Someone who isn't dead.

THE WASPORCIST
Amy Laurens

Today.

MY EARS WON'T STOP ringing. It's been a week now—ever since Halloween, actually. That party was insane. I prob'ly shouldn't have let that guy pour me a drink, even if he did compliment my outfit.

But anyway, the ringing. Every noise echoes in my left ear with a weird, computerized-voice-over effect. It's especially bad in a crowd, since the echoes get so loud I can't understand what anyone is saying.

I went to the doctor today. She says nothing's wrong. I think she thinks I'm making it up.

Nov 8.

Ear ringing persists. It's like the electricity in my brain is going mad, buzzing so loud I can hear it.

Will my brain explode, I wonder?

Day after yesterday.

The buzzing is so loud now I have trouble hearing anything else. At least it means I can't hear things echoing.

First day of the rest of forever, in which I never hear again.

Have determined that my brain has been replaced with a wasp, and it's mad at being trapped in my pitiful skull, hence continuous buzzing. Must see an insectologist or whatever they're called to get it out.

Nov 13.

It's Friday. I should have known that was a bad start. Insectologist, who is apparently actually called an entomologist, tells me that wasps don't live in people's heads. I told him I'm always an exception. He told me to call a shrink.

Had shrink. Didn't work. Besides, I don't need a shrink, I need a waspinator. I wonder what they're called. Let me check.

Internet says exterminator. How dull. I vote in favour of waspinator. Let me go call one.

Nov 13, later.

Called. Booked. Didn't tell the guy where the wasp was;

just said 'up there' when he asked. Hope he comes prepared.

Another day.

Waspinator should be coming today, wootwoo. I am so SICK of this buzzing. I swear, the thing is driving me insane. Even Josh thinks I'm acting weird, and he'd know, he's the King of Weird.

Oh, knock at the door. That'll be the Waspinator. I'll report back in a minute.

Later.

The guy looked at me like I was mad when I told him the wasp was in my head. "Too right it is," he said. I think that was a little uncalled for. Still, I made him check, just to be sure. He shone a light in through my ear and said he couldn't see anything that wasn't supposed to be there.

Personally, I'm suspicious. I think if I looked in *his* ear I wouldn't see anything at all. Ha. Idiot.

But seriously, what am I going to now? Who am I going to call?

...Who you gonna call? Ghost! Busters! Dun da-dun dun-dun.

HEY! That's actually not a bad idea! What if it's *not* a wasp? What if it's, like, a demon who's just *pretending* to be a wasp?

That's so awesome I'm practically bouncing in my seat. Who do you call for demons, again? Exercise-thingies. What are they called? Oh yeah, exorcists. Right.

Snigger. Wasporcists. That's what I need: a wasporcist. But I doubt that'll be in the phone book. I supposed I'll just try for a generic exorcist first.

I'll let you know how it goes, diary-m'dear.

Even later.

I love coincidence. Got this mad phone call earlier that Josh took. Sounded like it was one of those sales calls, you know? The ones where they try to sell you a trip to Hawaii or insurance for your fish or something? Yeah. Those. But anyway, I was listening, and so I heard when Josh told the guy we didn't need an exorcist.

I practically snatched the phone out of his hand, I was so excited. I mean, seriously? What are the odds?! So awesome. So anyway, exorcist—his name is Brad—agreed to come out. Says it sounds like it could be a demon. He gets situations like this all the time, he said.

Hmm. I wonder if there's, like, a conspiracy of demons, all invading people's heads as wasps? I wonder if Josh has heard buzzing lately?

I just ran out into the hall and asked him. He said he hasn't. Bummer. No conspiracy after all. Oh well. I guess I'll just wait for the exorcist.

Nov 20.

Exorcist is coming, exorcist is coming! I'm so excited. I hope he's cute.

He should be here any minute now—oh, look, see? A knock at the door. I wonder if he knew I was writing about him coming, and that's why he knocked now? I wonder if he's been waiting at the door for, like, half an hour, just waiting for me to sit down and start writing so he could knock just as I wrote about—

I'm COMING, Josh. Sheesh. Let a person finish their sentence, will ya?

Urgh, better go before he comes in here and see this. No one's supposed to know I'm keeping a journal. I'm only doing it 'cause the shrink last year said I should. Not that I ever have anything interesting to write about.

Well, until the wasp-invading-my-brain thing.

Bloody hell, Josh, COMING. Right. See me go...

Tonight.

OHMIGOSH! The Wasporcist is totally that guy from the party, you know, the random one who poured me a drink? And he's CUTE.

But yeah, ha, I told you it was a wasp-demon. Brad took one look and agreed. Said it was a pretty potent demon, though, so he'd have to come back a couple of times and have at it in bits—too strong to tackle all at once. Good thing I sold the car, exorcists aren't cheap.

Mind you, why would they be? With the work *they* have to do? No, thanks. Makes me shudder. I'm more than happy to pay someone else to do the dirty work. Especially if it means this infernal buzzing will stop.

Dec 2.

Sorry I haven't written in ages, diary-dearest. I've been... occupied. Don't tell Josh, but I think Brad—he's the exorcist I wrote about last time, remember?—I think he has a crush on me. He's come over every single day this week, usually while Josh's at work. He brought me flowers, yesterday. Daisies. My favourite, not that anyone but you knows that.

Josh says he's creepy. I dunno. He's pretty cute. And I think the buzzing isn't as bad when he's around.

scowl Josh still thinks I'm making it all up. Idiot. I bet he wouldn't even know what *colours* I like. (Green and purple, for the record.)

Anyway. Bed.

Dec 3.

I don't have long, I'm going out to dinner in a minute with—oh, better not say, just in case. I'm sure you can guess. We arranged it this morning when he came over. And guess what he brought with him? Earrings, purple and green ones. He's only known me for two weeks and already he knows more about me than stupid Josh.

Dec 6.

Brad is right. Josh is a dickhead. He's been totally unsympathetic about this whole wasp-demon head-invasion thing, and keeps on ragging at me for the money missing from our bank account. It's not like it's *that* much; Brad is charging me less than half price, since the demon's proving so hard to get rid of. And he told me at dinner the other night that he's barely had *any* clients this month, and he had to negotiate with his landlord to pay double rent for December because he couldn't afford to cover November.

...Maybe I *should* run away. I don't mind being poor. And I know what it's like to be so lonely...

But where can we go?

December nine, three nineteen pm. The moment of my momentous decision.

I'm doing it. Tonight. I'm going to sneak out of the house and I'll meet Brad and he'll take me away from here, away from all of this nonsense. The healing is almost complete, and he'll take me away, and then I'll be totally fixed, and he'll never be lonely again, and everything will be wonderful.

It's not like Josh will even care; he's barely spoken to me since he found me sitting in the corner the other day doodling hearts around Brad's name.

Okay, so that was a tactical mistake, but seriously, if he wasn't such a jerk I wouldn't be thinking of leaving.

No, not thinking, I *am* leaving. Tonight.

Oh, gosh, it gives me shivers just thinking about it. I'm so excited I can hardly wait! I wonder if Brad will mind if I'm early?

I'm going to go pack now, just in case. Can't wait can't wait can't WAIT!!!!

Josh closed the document, throat burning, chest tight. "Yes," he told the police officer standing behind him. "That's her diary."

"Well, you won't mind if we take the laptop up to the station as evidence then?"

Josh shook his head. What difference did it make?

The officer gave him a sympathetic look. "I'm truly sorry. But your help—well, it might just make the difference between finding the killer and not."

Josh nodded. Sure. Let them think he was a hero, if that's what they wanted. He knew the truth. He'd lost her long before some psycho had torn her body apart in the woods behind the house, and even long before she'd gotten that stupid idea about the wasp in her head.

The psychiatrist had warned him she might never come back. He'd been stupid to hope. And now his ear wouldn't stop ringing.

⌁⌁⌁⌁〰〰〰〰⋀〴〰〰〰⌁⌁⌁

AFTERMATH
Amy Laurens

"ARE YOU ALL RIGHT?"

I snorted. "Oh, yes. Absolutely."

Cran gave me a sidelong look. "I was only asking."

"And I was only answering." I shifted so's he couldn't see my face, and stared out the window. "Of course I'm fine. Why wouldn't I be? It was only a small demon, teeny tiny. Barely worth exorcising." My jaw twitched as I tried to hold back the sarcasm.

Silence for a moment, then I heard the rustle of cloth as he stood.

He left without saying a word.

I was glad.

I waited a while to be sure he wasn't coming back, then I went to the sideboard and poured myself a few too many finger-heights of lemon vodka. I glanced away so I didn't have to see my hands tremble.

I was fine. The demon was gone. It had needed barely any prompting, even; just a splash of holy water, a garlic sandwich and a quick prayer—gone.

A tiny demon.

Insignificant.

So why did I feel so damn messed up?

I gulped down the alcohol, ignoring the burn in my throat, and slumped back down on the lounge. I stared out the window, smiling half-heartedly as Molly-the-insane-labradoodle chased the neighbour's cat across the lawn.

Yesterday, if someone'd told me what was going to happen, I'd've called *them* insane. Actually, I'd've prob'ly called them a bloody idiot, get out of my way now, thanks very much. But whatever.

I closed my eyes and draped a hand over my face. The sunlight seemed extra bright and shiny today, and it hurt my eyes to look outside for long.

Something moved behind me and I jumped, whipping out the crucifix from down my shirt. "Dammit, Cran," I said. "Did you have to come in so suddenly like that?"

He looked abashed. "Sorry."

Cran never said sorry. My grip on the crucifix tightened and I found myself wishing I could switch my alco for water—the holy kind. "What did you say?"

He glanced up at me. "I said sorry. I know you're pretty jumpy still. I'll try to make more noise." He tried on a grin.

I narrowed my eyes. Was it just that my recent freak-out had put me on edge, or did something about him seem different to normal? A tightness around the eyes, a twitch of the lips, something in the carriage of his shoulders...

The crucifix dug into my palm. I set the drink down and shoved my hand into my pocket, looking for the last stray clove of garlic. It came up empty. Hell.

I edged towards the kitchen. "So, uh, big plans for today?" I asked.

Cran shrugged. "Game's on tonight, I was thinking of heading over to Mickey's to watch."

"Oh, yeah?" I said with deliberate casualness. The demon was good, very good. I could almost believe I was just making the whole thing up. If it hadn't just possessed me yesterday, if I hadn't seen its tics and mannerisms up close and personal, I'd've missed the whole exchange going on on Cran's face: demon versus man, the internal struggle for control.

"Yeah," the demon said with Cran's voice. "You?"

I stuck my bottom lip out nonchalantly. "Nothing much. Still, you know." I held up my free hand and stared at it, transfixed for a second by the shaking. *Bastard*, I thought. *You did this to me and you know it. I'll kill you this time. What was it that killed demons for good, again?*

Cran gave me a sympathetic look. "Yeah. That. Not much fun, I reckon."

I shrugged and made it to the kitchen, sliding in behind the bench and pretending I was rummaging for something to eat. "I lived," I said. *You won't,* I added in the privacy of my own skull—which, thank God, was private once again.

Bastard demon. First me, now Cran. It wasn't going to get away with this.

Stakes, that was it. Like vampires, their cousins. One big happy life-stealing family. I ground my teeth.

Cran moved toward me. "So how long do you think it will take? To, you know, recover?"

I fished around in the utensil drawer for the big bamboo chopsticks. A stick was nearly a stake, right? Near enough was good enough, or at least I bloody well hoped it would be. "No idea," I told Cran. "S'pose it depends."

"Yeah?" He—the demon—responded. "On what?"

I shrugged again. "Things."

"Can I help?"

Hell, he was right behind me. I could feel him breathing down my neck. I shivered. "Yeah," I said. "Yeah, you can."

He put his hands on my shoulders. "How?" His mouth was right next to my ear. His breath was warm.

F—ing bastard. Why Cran? Why the only man who'd ever loved me in my entire miserable life? Bloody, bloody hell. "Like this," I whispered.

I twisted around, one clean movement, too quick for him to react. The crucifix slammed into his forehead, the bamboo stake into the side of his neck.

His eyes went wide. "What the—"

He gurgled.

I pushed him off me and he crumpled to the floor, and I tried to pretend I wasn't crying. "You bastard," I said through the tightness in my throat. "I name you Azazel."

The air shimmered in front of me. "You rang?"

I blinked, regained my senses, scrambled backwards. "What the *hell*?"

The faint outline of the demon lifted an eyebrow. "You called. I appeared, despite the *warmth* of your reaction last time. To what do I owe the honour this time?"

My gaze flickered between the hazy demon, hovering in the middle of the kitchen, and the crumpled, broken body lying beneath it. "You possessed him. You bastard, you possessed the only man I ever loved!"

The demon glanced down. "That hunk of meat? Hardly. So few brain cells it would be like ingesting water to stave off famine. And the few that he has—had—were far too good to be pleasant." It shuddered. "No, thank you. I have better taste than that."

I stared. "No. You possessed him. I saw you!"

The demon huffed. "If you think, even for a *second*, that I would possess something like *that*..." It trailed off, head tilted, staring at the bamboo skewer in my hand.

I followed its gaze and stared horrified as the blood trickled down to meet my fingers.

"Oh, you didn't. You didn't!" The demon cackled. "Oh, my precious, that is just *too* lovely." It cackled louder. "Well done!"

I drew in a shaky breath. "Get lost," I said.

It clutched its sides, laughing uproariously.

"*Now,*" I said, anger hardening in my chest. I stood, took aim, threw the stake and the crucifix all at once.

The laughter cut off. The shimmer snapped out with a shriek.

I stared at the body lying glassy-eyed on the floor. The demon was gone.

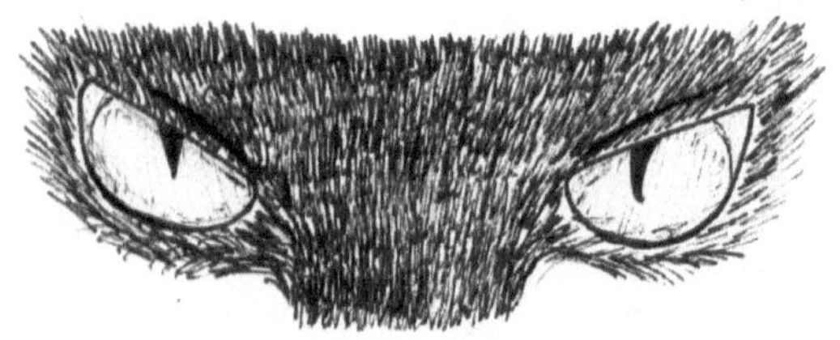

WHEN WAR CAME TO TOWN
Amy Laurens

WHEN THE WOMAN WITH flame-coloured hair rode into town on the demon horse, nobody knew it would happen. Sure, old Marley had just been ripped from his slumber in the room over the pub, dragged into the streets and flayed to within a half inch of death, but those kinds of things happened sometimes. All it took was a downturn in the economy, a few farms going sour, whispers in the wind of a witch, of black magic...

No. It was sad, ludicrous even, to think that people really thought Marley was clever enough for magic, but it wasn't the thing nobody knew could happen.

The bodies lining the street to see the woman, that was unexpected, the way they thrashed and elbowed and tromped, all trying to catch a brush of plate mail, or of the sharp, crackling hair of the deep-black horse. Unexpected, but also not that thing—not *It*. If people had stopped to think, they could have known she'd draw them to her like moths.

No. Not It.

The body, more meat now than human, with strips that hung from its limbs and a torso that still, days later, shuddered torturously in a parody of breathing as it lay caged over the square—that was a pity. Not a tragedy, because Virani had deserved, more or less, what he got—you don't steal from the Mayor's own treasury and deflower his teenage daughter without flirting with death as well. The flogging was perhaps a trifle unnecessary, as least to that degree. But still: not It.

Because the thing is, see, all these things are terrible. And if anyone had bothered to look into the eye of the demon horse as it pranced into town on Tuesday at dusk, they would have known immediately by the flicker of fire deep within that bad things were going to happen. And if they'd taken a moment to stare past the woman's captivating beauty with her deep brown skin and hair of flames, they would have seen not the same flicker in her eye, but something worse. Much worse.

And so really, all the violence? While it surely wasn't expected, it also wasn't surprising.

So what, then, was It? That one surprising thing that nobody knew would happen, than nobody could have predicted, that one thing that reminded everybody who they were and what really mattered?

That thing—it was Tikva.

Tikva, only seven, had joined the throng in the main street as the glorious woman on the coal-black horse had paraded past. She too had stretched out to brush finger against horsehair, and because of her small stature and resourcefulness in hiding behind an upturned crate, Tikva had succeeded where most others had not: she'd touched the demon horse. Her fingers had crackled against the deep black fetlock as though electricity bridged the gap between them, and Tikva was left cradling fingers slightly burned with heat and a memory slightly singed with hatred, both of which meant it was she who'd first warned her mother that the horse was a devil, and because her mother was the town's wisest Elder, the rest of the town had listened.

It hadn't lessened their fascination with the woman, of course, or the horse. But at least afterwards Tikva could say she'd told them so.

But the strangest part of touching the horse hadn't been the realisation that it was a demon. The strangest part was realising that one day she too would ride into town on a horse like this, and all the world would come to see her pass. She'd shaken her head, shoved aside memories and burned fingers, and gotten up. The crowds were closing now that the woman on the horse had passed. Tikva brushed the dirt from her undyed woollen tunic and pursed her lips. Mother needed to know about this.

That spark of connection when Tikva touched the demon horse was astounding, and by all rights and accounts it should never have happened—changing the course of history because it did—but still: not It. Strange coincidences are sometimes possible, after all, enough so that while people note them, they are not utterly discombobulated by them. Some degree of chance, it is accepted, is part of life. Thus, not It.

When Tivka told her mother about the woman on the horse, mother frowned as though she'd heard Tikva's father was back in town, and left the room abruptly to dig out her best shearing knife from the shed, oiling it with lavender and valerian before returning to sheathe it in the block in the kitchen, the kitchen wherein a steady troop of neighbours began and, in fact, continued until the moment Virani was condemned to be flogged in the square; wherein Tikva's night-time repose was plagued by feverish dreams in which she was torn from herself over and over and over again to be thrown into the heat of battle; and wherein she, Tivka, stood, a calm epicentre in the midst of terror, and let the desire to fight wash over her.

It was some days since that first meeting when Tikva was sent down to the shop to buy more carrier oil for her mother, who had sold out of her famous calming tonic. Tikva eased her way down a street full of scowl-faced villagers, all ready to bite at each other at the least provocation, and climbed the steps to the shopfront with much relief.

Midway along, something nipped at her skirts. Tikva turned to see the demon horse tethered to the hitching post, being given an extra wide berth by patrons and street traffic alike. Tikva craned her neck to and fro, but there was no sign of the red-haired woman who'd brought trouble upon the town (so her mother said, and so Tikva felt it to be true).

Lip consideringly between her teeth, Tikva stared at the great black stallion. The electric spark she'd felt last time—*had* it been a coincidence? And if so, did it still matter? And if not, then... what? Breath held in her too-tight throat, Tivka reached for the horse.

His nostrils flared and his eyes rolled. Great, square teeth the colour of blood-stained bone nipped at her. Tikva sniffed and rapped the stallion's nose. "No."

He stilled, snorting and shivering, ears flickering as he waited for her touch.

Tikva gave a satisfied nod and rubbed her thumb over the soft, delicate velvet of his nose. "Much better."

Footsteps sounded on the wooden steps and Tikva leapt away from the horse. She whirled and entered the shop before she could see who it was, hustling towards the oils with great concentration.

As Tikva neared the counter, Mister Avery lifted his green-striped apron from the vast expanse of his belly and wiped his face. "Well," he said gravely. "That is a concern."

"What's a concern?" Tikva asked in the tone of someone thirty years older and with as much expectation of being answered. Being her mother's daughter had its benefits.

"Virani was found with Miss Allum," Mistress Spector said, bosom heaving as she rearranged it on the counter. "And a rather large suitcase of the Mayor's own funds. The court has ruled for immediate flogging to be followed by imprisonment in the cage until death."

Tikva felt the blood drain from her face. This, this was the thing she'd been waiting for all week without ever knowing it; this was the culmination of all the whispered mutterings, the fights, the tiffs, the quarrels; this was the powder keg now lit, and someone had to stop it.

The bottles of oil clunked to the floor and rolled away under a shelf, unheeded.

But this was not It, because that thing we are waiting for, that It, was unexpected, and Tivka herself had known that something like Virani's flogging would be the natural outcome of the flame-haired woman's influence.

As Tikva approached the square, she knew she was too late; the shouts of the whip master mingled with the agonised cries of Mister Virani, both a counterpoint to the bass harmony of the crowd's jeers.

Tikva jostled her way through until she could see the flogging post. For a brief instant, her stomach churned, but then she reminded herself that she'd seen worse out back of the butchers, and almost as bad on her mother's healing bench, where often she'd assisted. He shouldn't have tried to run away with Miss Allum—not this week, at any rate. Stupid, stupid man.

The whip master raised his hand to strike again at a thing already more flesh and bone than man. "No. Enough." Barely anyone in the crowd heard Tikva, and they never understood the authority of her words until much, much later, but at Tikva's command, the whip master froze. Beneath him, Virani shuddered and moaned, and for a moment there was a hush.

Then the crowd began to shout. "Why did you stop? Keep going! He's not had even two hundred yet, come on! Is your arm tired? I'll do it! Come on! Flog him some more!"

Tikva closed her eyes against tears that threatened to drown her fury, and reached out to the anger that filled the crowd. Softly, she began to sing.

Peace, my child, now will rest
Upon your head while bluebirds sleep
Close your eyes and be you blessed
For peace abides here river-deep.

The words of the song unfurled through the crowd like blossoms, and slowly, one by one, people began to sing with Tikva.

It was only when the whole crowd lifted their voices together and Tivka could feel the harmony emanating from them that she released the whip master. He collapsed to the ground, shuddering, tears gushing from his guilt.

The demon horse pranced into the middle of the square, and the red-haired woman stared imperiously down from its back. "Who dares halt justice?"

Tikva tossed her head and marched forward, halting with folded arms in front of the horse she had no fear of. "I am the one you seek."

The woman on the horse started visibly as she stared down at the tiny creature in front of her, thin and small boned. She laughed, a sound that set the men in the crowd on their toes and the women on the arms of their men. "You are not the one."

Tikva tossed her head again for good measure. "Look me in the eye," she told the woman, "and tell me I am not."

Still laughing, the woman dismounted and strode forward, reins looped casually in one hand, hair rippling like flames in the breeze. She knelt down in front of Tikva, a smile dancing, and looked deep into Tikva's eyes.

Tivka knew the moment when the woman recognised her for what she was: the woman's eyes tightened, the fire dampened, and her whole body went stiff. "No," the woman whispered. "You cannot be she."

Tivka smiled, and it was the smile of swamp crocodiles when they corner unwary prey. "Oh yes," she whispered. "I am she." And although she did not fully know what it meant, she knew without a doubt that it was true.

The woman stumbled in getting to her feet and stepped back a few paces before bowing curtly. "My Sister."

Tivka nodded in return, for even though her power was newly arrived, sparked into life by contact with the demon horse and matured by her act in halting the whip-bearer, it bore with it all the knowledge of the centuries; she could feel all the others before her who had worn the mantle of Peace, and she knew the truth of War's greeting: they were sisters now indeed. "Sister."

She send a trickle of her power outwards, probing at the edges of War's defence, and although they were locked as ever in a battle between two equals, she knew that right now, at this time, in this place, the battle was hers to win.

The other woman knew it too, and stepped back once again. "What do you wish done?" she asked, not deferential, but without the earlier command.

"You will go," said Tikva, a fact stated as simply as the colour of the sky, not a request, not an order. "And you will not return."

The woman nodded. "And him?" She gestured to the tattered lump of flesh that once might have been called Virani.

"He will hang in the cage, as the law decided," Tikva replied.

Around her, people muttered, and the woman called War raised her eyebrows. "From you, Sister? That is not what I would have expected."

"Peace too has a price," Tikva said in a voice that could sharpen diamonds, gaze never leaving the red flame eyes of War. "And this is my town."

War stared back thoughtfully for a long moment, then nodded. "I'll see you again one day," she said before swinging up onto her demon stallion.

"When you do," said Peace, "I will have a horse too. And I'll know how to fight."

War chuckled, a sound for their ears alone, and reached out to ruffle Peace's hair. "I'm sure you will," she said, not unkindly. "I look forward to it. Until next time, then," she added as she straightened in the saddle.

Peace nodded, jaw clenched tightly. "Until next time."

War's demon stallion reared his farewell, then galloped off into the gathering gloom.

Peace looked around the square at her town, and told them sternly: "Go home, and stop being ridiculous. I'll deal with you all in the morning."

The town, bowing to the wishes of a seven-year-old girl, recognising the authority of a millennia-old Power, did, and in the morning Tikva told them off, and that, of course, was It, because nobody could have predicted when War rode in that she would meet her match in a back-country town in the middle of nowhere, in the shape of a seven-year-old girl—and yet, she did. It.

THE LIES WE KNOW
Liana Brooks

"REMEMBER, YOU'RE ALL GOING to die eventually. Might as well make it worthwhile."

As pep talks went, the commander's was down with the likes of 'Let's all get killed!', but he seemed convinced he had a point. The problem was, he didn't. I knew he was wrong. My whole life had proved him wrong.

Most people died eventually. But life is all about probability and statistics. There are no absolutes. Even death, a penultimate absolute that claims 99.999999% of the population, isn't truly an absolute. There's always that .000001%. Me.

Everyone clamped their helmets tight shut against the vacuum of space. We were going into battle against overwhelming odds and we needed to make them underwhelming odds before the Kanfir ships reached the jump for the Euon Ri system.

Thirty-seven hours later, I was the only survivor, and the captured Kanfir flag ship was arguing with me.

"I cannot obey that order."

"Kendla sentient ship! I don't care what you think you can or cannot do, change course before we hit the sun!"

"I cannot obey that order. A senior line officer must enter the course change into the log book."

I banged my head on the soft, somewhat gummy edge of the ship's interface. "Is there a senior line officer left alive?"

"No."

Didn't think so. The Kanfir hadn't anticipated us swarming their ships with soldiers in aerial jets meant for orbital station work. The barges had closed, we'd shot off across the vacuum, and watched the empty barges burn behind us. It was a suicide mission. Sort of. Not for me, per se, but for everyone else. "Are there any junior officers left alive?"

I didn't want to go into the sun, but this ship was the last one left with working navigation controls. Sort of. The Kanfir captain had burned the override interface before we took their control room, but the ship itself was alive. I didn't know enough about the Kanfir to know if the ship was a species they'd caught and enslaved, or if they'd created these behemoths in some lab, but whatever the creature's history, it was bent on driving me to insanity.

"I can find no junior officers," the ship reported, sounding ever-so-slightly distressed.

"Go down the chain of command and let me know when you find someone who can be promoted to senior line officer in the event of catastrophic loss of life."

"I have three thousand nine hundred and seventeen individuals who fit those parameters."

"Is one of them alive?"

The ship was silent for a moment. "Yes."

I looked up at the amber brown hull in surprise. "On this ship? Alive?"

"Yes."

"Where?" I checked the charge on my gun. Still above thirty percent. Good enough for government work.

"Second Sergeant Bradford Rios is in temporary stasis in medical hold twenty-nine B," the ship said.

"Is that the medical ward with a hole gaping into the vacuum of space?"

"Yes." There was a cricket chirp and the ship added. "Should I focus repair energies on that ship section?"

Ten days until we hit the critical point of maneuvers and were too close to the sun to escape.

"Sure. Repair away. Let me know when I can go rescue the new commanding officer."

<hr>

Eight days later, I'd reached a wary understanding with the ship. It gave me correct information promptly, and I didn't stab it with an electroblade.

Electroblades are antique—kind of like me. Illegal just about everywhere I've been, but they're so rare that no one bothers to ask if you're carrying one. No sentient alive likes their flesh sliced while electricity floods their system. It's horribly painful, leaves scars that take decades to heal, and memories that never fade. Ask me how I know.

"Moira?" the ship said as I heaved another oversized Kanfir body into the airlock I was using as a dumping ground. Whatever they'd been feeding these boys, it was heavy in protein. Felin heavy bodies, all muscle and nice to look at—but pretty didn't stop bullets and it didn't make my disposal job any easier.

I slammed my fist against the lock plate. "Yes?"

"Medical hold twenty-nine B is secured and airtight. Would you like me to begin recovery of Second Sergeant Bradford Rios?"

"Yes please."

There was the cricket-like chirp I'd come to dread; the ship had found something that was going to cause an argument. "Second Sergeant Bradford Rios is under stasis lock for another ninety-two years, by the ship's working calendar."

I raised an eyebrow. "What for?"

"Treason, disobedience to a direct order, questioning a superior officer, blasphemy, violence, obstruction of justice, drunk or disorderly conduct, seventeen weapons infractions involving possession of a weapon or device of non-regulation origin, four weapons infractions involving discharge of a deadly weapon in a restricted area, fourteen weapons infractions involving failure to pass mandatory weapons inspections, and failure to complete a five kilometer run in under twenty minutes standard."

"Sounds like a real gem," I said. "Wake our boy up and let him know that he has been promoted to senior captain of the fleet."

"Admiral," the ship corrected. "But I do not believe the Second Sergeant can obtain the rank of Admiral with these charges against him. It's unprecedented."

"Did you find another beating heart on this tugboat?"

"Only you." The ship might have been a fleshy AI, but it made 'you' sound like the foulest curse word in the galaxy.

"Well then, it's me or your Boy Wonder for fleet admiral. Who would you rather answer to?"

"Beginning defrost sequence for Fleet Admiral Bradford Rios," the ship said quickly. "Estimated conscious alertness in thirty-eight minutes."

"Plenty of time."

I tidied up, dumped the bodies out the airlock, sorted hand weapons and other gewgaws I'd stripped off the dead, and wandered down to the newly-restored medical bay.

I had to get myself one of these ships. Self-repairing battleship? Be still my cold heart! No matter how well built a ship was, it eventually fell apart. Time destroyed things. Most things. I'd watched cultures rise and fall. Empires that came and went in the blink of an eye. Sometimes really in the blink of an eye. Most revolutions don't last more than a year or two, something historians forget because a year of anarchy always feels like an eternity.

The ship's medical hold was a barracks-style room with several dozen medical cots separated by membranous tissue the same amber-gold as the rest of the ship's interior. Before alpha battalion had punched a hole in the side, there'd probably been blankets, hand-held medical scanners, and the rest of the usual doctor paraphernalia. Now there was a Kanfir man in a clean engineering sergeant's uniform lying on a silver table, lips tinged blue.

"He is alive still, right? You didn't wake him up wrong?"

"The stasis chamber was below optimal temperature when the skitters retrieved the fleet admiral," the ship replied, "but he is within recovery range."

"Not brain dead?"

"There is a forty percent chance of brain damage with this procedure."

Not that the ship or I were likely to notice unless the damage left him drooling. Rios hadn't sounded like he was firing all pistons up top to begin with.

"Do you have a blanket or anything? He looks cold."

A cricket chirp. "Internal sensors cannot find anything similar to a blanket onboard. The stores room was completely destroyed, as were the barracks."

A lucky hit. We'd caught the Kanfir ground forces sleeping in their bunks while the zoomies swatted at space gnats. Fly boys couldn't fight hand-to-hand like the infantry, not without a few drinks on them, and the loss of the entire infantry force of Kanfir in a single hit was more demoralizing to them than I'd expected.

"Fleet Admiral Rios is waking," the ship reported.

I turned to my new comrade at arms. Time to play nice.

⁓⁓⁓

Ford blinked his eyes at the harsh light. There was a little knick in the lamp cover. Either he'd been dragged out of stasis sleep on the Subtle Queen or someone had put up a fight going down. Icy nightmares clung in his mind. Shadows tugged at him even now—the last of the stasis drugs burning out of his body he hoped. Stasis was hell.

"Wakey wakey, Admiral," a sardonic female voice said.

He turned, expecting to see one of her majesty's own medtechs, and instead saw a girl no more than twenty, wearing blood-red space armor and flipping a knife with a blade made of lightning. Fleet had clearly changed in the ninety-five years he'd spent tied in the shadows.

She winked at him. "How you feeling?"

Ford sat up slowly. The shadows tried to drag him down, but he made it upright. "Nauseous."

"I hear that happens after stasis."

He looked around the empty medical hold. "Doctor?"

The stranger shook her head. "Long story. Let's focus on the positive things, okay? Like your promotion."

Straight to her majesty's own slave mine. Ford grunted and watched the woman sheath her knife.

"You are the new fleet admiral." Her smile was cheerful and youthful, wholly at odds with her body language.

He smiled mirthlessly. "I wouldn't be promoted to anything in fleet unless everyone died, and even then it would be a long shot."

She nodded. "Funny story that. I'll tell you as we walk."

Ford tried to stand. The floor felt alien under his socks. "I need boots."

"What size?"

"Nine and three-quarters."

"Do you mind if they have blood on them?" She looked perfectly serious.

"Why not get them from ship stores?"

She wrinkled her nose. "There's a tiny problem with the ship stores."

"Queenie?" Ford said, calling for the ship.

"Fleet Admiral Rios?" the Subtle Queen replied evenly in Her Majesty's voice.

He shook his head. Unbelievable. "Queenie, may your humble penitent retrieve new boots and gear from the ship's stores?"

"Request denied," the Queen said.

"The ship doesn't have stores," the girl added. "There's a gaping hole where the blankets used to be."

"And where are the Queen's Men?" Ford asked.

"Dead." The girl shrugged.

The cold shock rolled over him in a soft wave. It wasn't wholly unexpected. Only total devastation would bring the fleet to need him as a soldier of any kind. "What happened to them?" Famine? Attack? Another internal coup between rival princesses?

"Me, mostly." The girl smiled. "You can call me Moira."

He stared at her childlike face. "You?"

"Like I said, long story. Now, let's walk over to the control room, and you can tell the ship to change course so we don't run into the sun. Then we'll have a nice long talk about astrochartography, political realities, and the chances of you living to see another meal. M'kay?"

Possibilities and theories free-wheeled through his mind until Ford caught hold of one reality. "We're diving into the sun?"

"Yes, and we have less than forty-eight hours to correct course before we're stuck with it. If you can't get the ship to obey, I'm going to need some time to find another way to reprogram this beast."

Ford stopped short. "You can't reprogram a celestial queen! She responds only to the voice of Her Majesty or the Queen's Men who fight for her life and honor!"

Moira looked unmoved. "I know where the brain center is. Talk the ship into changing course, or your queen gets a lobotomy."

Ford stared at her. "Are all women like you?"

"All the women you need to worry about."

The former sergeant wasn't happy with his sudden change of rank. His body language shifted as we walked down the deserted halls, still splashed with dried blood. In the medical hold he'd been depressed but mostly relaxed, reacting slowly. The further we walked, the tenser he became. Muscles bunched up in his shoulders. His fists curled. His stride became a defiant march past the field of battle now a week old.

"They're all dead?"

"It was the Kanfir or the Euonians." I shrugged. "That's the thing about wars. People die."

He shook his head. "It wasn't war. Her Majesty's children required new suns to graze near. The fleet was called to search the star paths for the coming swarm."

"Swarm? Like... insect swarm?"

He frowned. "Know you nothing of the Kanfir?"

"Hyper-violent male race with enslaved females kept locked on their home planet. You guys come in, kill everyone, and then abandon the systems you've destroyed."

He stopped walking and stared.

I rolled my eyes. "I've seen it done in Gretchuia and Rison. Don't deny it. I saw the senate house of Dreul when you were done in the Gretchuia system. There was nothing left. Even the stones were dust."

"Because Her Majesty ordered the place prepared for her brood!" he protested. "Her Majesty called. We cannot disobey her will."

"You need a new government," I said.

He shook his head violently this time. "No. No. You mistake me. Us. Her Majesty owns us. We are the Queen's Men. We cannot disobey. Not 'We don't think about disobeying', or 'We don't want to disobey', or 'We all agree with Her Majesty'. We cannot go against her. She is the Life Giver and the Life Taker. There is no way but hers. When she wishes to lay a clutch, we obey and clear land, and now her daughters seek to swarm, to take suns of their own. We obey or we die."

"Or you obey and still die." I smiled. "Looks like a lose-lose situation all around." I led him to the control room. "Does this whole queen business mean I can't take over the ship at all, ever?"

"The ship is the Subtle Queen. It is a piece of Her Majesty, and extension of her will and dominion."

"I'm not actually hearing a no here."

The sergeant stalked over to the control console and stared. "I was never trained for this."

"No worries. I know what I'm doing." I showed him how to call up the screen and set various coordinates.

"I should take us home," he said.

I shook my head. "Bad idea. At home you still have a prison sentence to live out. Let's go somewhere fun. Escinia is nice this time of year. Or the Sertian colonies. I hear they're making great progress with the swamp plagues. We can go, find new jobs, loiter on a beach somewhere, make new friends... It'll be great!"

He stared at her. "These are not places I have ever heard of."

"Again, no worries. When I was growing up I'd never heard of them either." I gave him the coordinates to Sertian space. They were a disorganized group with multiple governments on each of their three settled planets and they promised to have an interesting future. It was somewhere a person could get lost in the tides of humanity.

The sergeant sat reluctantly, then turned. "Where were you born? Far from here? On Dreul perhaps?"

"I was born in San Francisco on this cute little planet called Earth."

He frowned. "That is an Elder Planet, one long forgotten, the Star Paths to it closed."

I shrugged. "I didn't say I was born recently. I mean, when I was a kid the big excitement was that man had walked on the moon. Interstellar travel was a fiction then." I snorted in amusement. "I thought driving eight hours to see my grandma on holidays was a big adventure because we crossed a desert."

"But... you're a child!" He held his hand near my head. "You're not grown yet."

I smiled. "I'm short. I'm not a kid."

"You are still young."

"Younger than the universe maybe, but not as young as I look." I sat down in the first officer's chair. "I visited Dreul when they were building the senate house. That was nearly three hundred years ago. I remember the system was found by a probe from Xalian. It was all over the news for months. New world found! Habitable planet! Everyone was so excited and then there were arguments over whether the Xalian river gods approved of Dreul. Once they found the gold river it was fine, of course. Obviously a heaven planet. People rioted for a chance to go. The murder rate sextupled overnight. Crazy times."

Rios sat beside me in the captain's chair. "You learned all this as a child?"

"I lived all that as an adult. An old woman. Very old." I shrugged.

"You don't look old."

"Aging is the decay of telomeres. Your body stops replicating the cells correctly. Mutations take over. You fall apart. You die. I don't. I have no cellular mutations."

"That's very strange."

"Truly freakish," I agreed.

"Impossible," the ship chimed in. "There is no similar anomaly on record."

I looked at the amber ceiling. "How many times was I shot during the initial assault on this vessel?"

"Nineteen direct hits recorded," the ship said petulantly.

"Do we need to have another talk about behaving?" I flipped open my electroknife.

There was a cricket chirp from the ship. "No."

"Didn't think so."

I smiled for the Kanfir's benefit. "Don't worry about it. I'm a freak. I was born this way. I'd say I'll die this way, but, well, that'd be a lie."

"It seems many things in life are lies," he murmured.

For a moment I wondered if I'd have to use the electroblade on him to get him to cooperate, but abruptly he placed both hands on the console.

He smiled at me, a toothy, hungry thing that hardened his eyes. "And you'll show me the universe," he said.

My own smile stretched wider in response. "I'll show you the universe."

"Then I'd better turn us around."

As he reset the course, I sighed and felt the knots in my shoulders begin to release. I'd show him the universe, alright. This boy was in for the wildest ride of his life.

ANYTHING FOR YOU
Amy Laurens

I TURNED TO JACQUIE and tilted my head under the bright dressing room lights. "What do you think?" I knew her too well to think she'd lie.

Her face fell. "Oh, honey. That colour is all wrong for you!"

My stomach sank. "What? No! I asked the woman at the counter! She did a skin test and everything!" I whirled back to the mirror and scrutinised my jawline. Sure enough, if I craned my neck up and tilted to the right, a line of orange traced my jaw from chin to earlobe. "What am I going to do?" I turned to Jacquie in a panic. "The formal's in"—I checked the big old train station clock on the wall—"three hours and I have a hair appointment and I have to get dressed and we have to drive there, and besides all that, I'm broke!" I buried my hands in my face and tried to pretend I wasn't sobbing over makeup. After all, children in Africa were dying. Children in Africa weren't preparing simultaneously for their senior formal *and* their first date with the love of their high school life though, to be fair.

"Return it," Jacquie said. "It's the only thing you can do."

"It's opened!" I wailed. "They'll never take it back! I'm broken! The whole evening is ruined!"

Jacquie took me by the arm and marched me to the door as I waved the open tube of foundation vaguely. "You've clearly never seen me negotiate," she promised as we climbed into the car. "Don't worry. Everything will be fine. You know I'll do anything to make this date perfect for you. It's going to be fine."

✳✳✳

We waited as the shop assistant served three other people ahead of us. Finally, it was our turn.

"How may I help you?" the perfectly-coiffed woman asked, her blonde hair piled atop her head and flawless makeup smoothing her cheeks.

Jacquie pinned her with a steely stare. "We need to exchange some makeup," she said firmly, placing the tube down on the table.

The woman gave it a cursory glance and plastered a false smile in place. "I'm sorry, this has been opened. No returns on opened items."

Jacquie plunked our ace down on the table: the list on store letterhead detailing the makeup the previous assistant had recommended for me. "In this case," she said, "I believe you should make an exception. As you can see, the colour"—she squinted at the list—"*Sharryn* recommended for my friend is all wrong."

The store woman glanced at me and I tilted my head obligingly, clearly revealing the line of orange along my jaw that we'd left in place for evidence. She frowned. "Well. I am sorry about this, and you can be certain that Sharryn will be reprimanded. In cases such as this it is sometimes possible to make an exchange, but I'm afraid you've purchased Hellfire foundation. Did you read the fine print at all?" she added with the scathing tone of one used to dealing with idiots on a regular basis.

Stomach fluttering with trepidation, I shook my head. She handed back the list and I skimmed to the bottom of the page. The usual disclaimers were there, indemnifying the store against skin damage, allergic reactions and so forth—and there, right at the end, in print so tiny I had to hold the paper an inch from my nose to read it, a final clause: Purchasers agree that along with any financial exchange the store sees fit to apply, all purchases of Hellfire products shall paid for with the irredeemable giving over of the purchaser's soul. Purchases of Hellfire products are final, non-refundable, and non-exchangeable, except where a soul of greater value may be applied with the willing consent of the soul-owner.

Great. Where was I going to get a willing soul of greater value at such short notice? I pressed the list to my forehead and sighed. There was *one* option, of course... "Jacquie?"

"What is it? Why can't you exchange it?" She peered worriedly at me, brown eyes wide.

My heart pounded. "You know how you owe me that favour?"

Her brow creased. "Well sure. But—"

"Would you be willing to do it for me now?" I said, cutting over her.

"Um, yes? I guess so. I don't know how that will help, though." She turned to the shop woman, puzzled.

The woman lifted a considering eyebrow at me.

"Well?" I said. "She's willing. Hers is of greater value, isn't it?" Of course it was; Jacquie was an angel. I, on the other hand, was self-evidently not.

The woman's other eyebrow joined the first. "Yes." She turned to Jacquie. "If you'll just come with me, Miss, I'm sure we can get this all sorted out."

"Um, okay?" Jacquie shot me a puzzled glance before following the shop assistant out the back.

I smiled and nodded encouragingly. "Thank you!" I called. "Thank you so much!" I couldn't give up my first date with Matt. He was the love of my high school life, after all. Jacquie would understand. Eventually.

SAVED

Liana Brooks

HIS FEET DANGLED OVER the abyss. Somewhere far below was the path down to the village. Heavy spring fog hid the trees and the gargoyles that guarded the ancient castle. His fingers squeaked against stone as he slipped. Only a matter of time: leg bleeding, out of breath, stripped of wand and magic... Yes, he was going to die. It didn't matter that he'd beat the nightmare beast. In the end—

"That looks terribly uncomfortable."

He looked up through the mist to see an unfamiliar face. Not wholly unfamiliar; he'd seen her in classes and wandering the halls. Princess Something-That-Sounded-Like-A-Bird; he'd never learned her name. He assumed she was one of the shy, retiring girls who saw magical training as a good way to meet a potential husband. Since he wasn't shopping for a ball-and-chain, he'd avoided her. "Help?"

"However did you get in this predicament?" she asked, not even bothering to reach for him.

"Long story." His fingers burned as he slipped another centimeter towards death.

She shrugged. "Go on and tell me, then. I have nothing better to do this evening."

Blasted chit! Was that a subtle dig at the fact that nearly everyone else was at his best friend's party? "Pull me up!"

"I think not." She stepped away and he slipped, felt gravity pulling him down, saw death coming for him... and fell on the battlements at the feet of the girl. The modest green dresses she favored in class had been replaced by a wider skirt and a much more revealing bodice. And from this angle, he could see she was barefoot. Not exactly what he'd expected from one of the meek-and-mild types.

He pushed himself up. "So. Thank you."

She raised an eyebrow. "Story?"

"I was attacked by an iffrit. You know the ones with the pointy tails with the poison? I saw it skulking around and thought it was going after Rena and Lakis." He shrugged. Bjorn Lakis and he had been friends since they were only interested in chasing frogs and wallowing in mud. The announcement of Lakis's ascent to his family's throne and the subsequent engagement to his sweetheart of three years was a good reason to celebrate, and a wonderful opportunity for foes to attack. Out of habit, he'd taken the task of watching Lakis's back.

The girl walked around him, long skirt swirling as the fog poured over the crenelations. "An iffrit?"

"Yes."

"Long way for an iffrit to fly. They are desert dwellers, and I can't see them hunting this far north."

"Someone could have summoned it. Or someone might keep an iffrit as a pet. You never know."

"Neat trick if they did." She tilted her head to the side, her gaze focused on his leg. "You should tend to that before you bleed to death."

"Right. I'll just pluck a bandage from nowhere, shall I?"

She waved her hand and he felt the warmth of a healing spell creep over him.

No wand, and she'd done two major spells. He tucked that bit of information away to chew on later. "Thank you."

"You should get back to the party. They'll miss you."

"Uh-huh." He hesitated. "Are you coming?"

"I wasn't invited." Her jaw clenched. Her dark eyes flashed. "I'm from a minor kingdom. No one heeds us."

The hair on the back of his neck rose up. This is how people wound up with cursed castles and daughters sleeping for a hundred years. "Lakis had an open invitation to everyone. There weren't formal invites."

"Lakis doesn't know my name."

He didn't know her name. A clue: half his childhood had been spent memorizing the names of every royal family in the kingdoms. Names, histories, birthdates... By the time he'd arrived at school to finish his formal magical and political training, he already knew the names by heart.

She wore colors from one of the smaller kingdoms— green and silver and snake-eye yellow at times—but he didn't know her name. "Lakis forgets his own name at times," he hedged as he wracked his brain for the answer. "Your kingdom has friendly relations with his. You should come." He tried a friendly smile.

She was smirking. An intolerable 'I know something you never will' smirk that set his teeth on edge.

And, heaven's fire, but the fog was building now. They were caught in a cloud bank and if thunder didn't roll and echo across the stone work of the castle soon, he'd eat his boots. Where'd the storm come from anyway? His eyes narrowed suddenly. "You're not a princess."

Hers went wide with practiced innocence. "What?"

"I know them all. I don't know you. And storm magic isn't something you find in the royal families. Especially in inbred little kingdoms. Weather magic isn't good for much. No one breeds for it. So you're either a bastard, or…"

The idea that hit him square in the head was unthinkable. The castle was *the* place to send magical, royal off-spring. No one came without a hand-written invitation with heavy gilding on it. There might be a few minor nobles, and one or two bastards had walked the halls, but always as part of someone's political long game. The unthinkable—that a commoner had come of her own accord—was too much.

But the storm was curling around her, the clouds seeping into her and moving with her. She raised an eyebrow. "You were going to say?"

"Why aren't you beating men back with a stick?" That was not what he'd meant to say, but the words had tumbled out of their own accord.

And she was laughing. "Why would they notice me?"

"Rarity value! Look at you, a sorceress with no political or familial ties."

"Mmm, bad for networking."

"But good for removing embarrassing genetic diseases and having a wedding that won't start a war." He stopped and considered this. "No one has noticed you yet?"

"If I hadn't wandered up here to see the storm, would you have noticed me?"

"No. I would have died."

She rolled her eyes. "You know what I mean."

"Eventually. Probably. I've seen you in class." He considered this. "You're always so quiet."

"If I stood out, people would ask questions."

"Fair enough. I won't ask questions. I only have one—singular—as it is."

Her spine stiffened and her fingers curled tightly. "Ask."

"Want to go on a date with me?"

THE OTHER CARLY
Amy Laurens

THE DOOR TO MY hiding place slid open and I burrowed deeper under my arms against the tabletop.

"Joanna Richards," said a voice that was whisperingly familiar. "My how the mighty do fall."

Footsteps, then a warm pressure against my side. I cracked an eyelid open to peek at the boy from under my arm. Decently-muscled shoulder, longish neck, dark hair... My eyebrows lowered. I couldn't see his face, but that jawline definitely reminded me of someone.

He shifted. "You've grown up."

Ah. Not a boy. Ryan. I sighed and pressed my face back against the cool of the counter. "If you've come to patronise me, don't. My day has been shite enough as it is."

He was quiet for a second, then drew a little away. "Sorry. I didn't mean it like that. It's just, the last time I saw you, you were twelve and berating the house mistress who tried to punish you for shinning out the dorm window." He snickered, then gave a contented little sigh. "Her face is etched into my memory for all time."

In spite of myself, I smiled a little. "Yeah. That was a good moment."

"Yeah." He drifted away for a moment into a happy little reverie. "But anyway, moving on. What's up with you? Why are you in here? I thought we only used this place when the parents came to visit." He sat bolt upright. "They're not in town, are they? Because my folks are with me, and if—"

I pushed myself out of my slump and rolled my neck. "Dude, chill. No parents. It's fine."

His brow wrinkled. "Then why are we in here?"

I shrugged one shoulder and stared at a stain on the counter. "I went to Carly Davies' party today."

Ryan raised an eyebrow. "We like her now?"

"Pft." I cut him a look. "What do you take me for?"

"So why did you—Oh." Glum understanding clouded his face. "It goes like this: you pick someone easy—"

"Hey!"

"Alright, someone you were friends with then, a long, long time ago, but who saw you once for what you really are and did the smart thing and ditched you. Only you can't believe that's true, even now, and so you invite them, and beg and plead, and promise you'll be friends again, that you've seen the error of your ways and if only they would *just come* to your *party*," Ryan said in his best falsetto, clasping his hands under his chin and fluttering his eyelashes, "the rainforests will stop disappearing and climate change will be averted. Only then, when they come, you laugh. You laugh loud and long, and all your cronies laugh too, and you tell yourself that they deserve it because they ditched you—but really it's because you're empty inside." He straightened. "Am I right?"

My lips twisted as I swallowed a chuckle. I'd forgotten how easily he could wring laughter from me. I made a note to let him do it again sometime. "Close," I said. "Or you could just invite the whole year on Facebook and then, when your stupid ex-friend's curiosity gets the better of her and she shows up—*then* you laugh." I gave Ryan a wry smile. "Pretty dumb, huh."

Ryan nudged my shoulder with his. "No. Not dumb."

I dangled my feet off the edge of the chair and stared at the tiles. For a second—no, less than that, half a second—for half a second when I'd arrived at Carly's giant, white-picketed, tall-oaked, gable-roofed mansion of perfection, it had felt like old times, like I was six again and nothing else in the world mattered except that I was about to walk into the most amazing house I'd ever seen in my life. For just that half second, I could imagine what a friendship between a grown-up Carly and a grown-up Joanna might look like.

And then Maddy had spotted me, looked me up and down as she towered below me on stilettos longer than my arms that allowed her to just scrape five foot, and she'd said the fatal words, and the whole party had turned to give me that look, one part shocked, two parts cruel mockery, and four parts like the most disgusting insect in the world had stood up and spoken.

Although given Carly was scared of moths and thought they were putrid, and given I kind of liked them, all cute and fuzzy with feathery antennae as they were, that bit could have been worse. I sighed.

"Come on," said Ryan, grabbing my hand and hauling me to my feet. "Let's go eat some ice cream."

⁕⁕⁕

I stared glumly at my bowl, chinking my spoon absently against my water glass. Not even peach and coconut gelato had been able to lift my mood.

Ryan shifted, and as I glanced up he caught my eye. "There is this one thing," he said slowly, as though the words were heavy and fragile and had to be put down with great care.

"What one thing?" I was pretty sure nothing he could suggest would make me happier today, but it was sweet of him to try.

When he met my eyes again, his were aflame. "I've learned things since I've been gone. I can control it now. You could have it—revenge."

I shrugged, feigning nonchalance because the burn that started with that word seemed too terrible to own. Revenge. Eight long years of petty hatreds stacked themselves up and up until Carly's head toppled from them all. Goosebumps rose on my arms; I told myself it was only the unfortunate combination of ice cream and aggressive air conditioning.

"Well?"

Ryan's cheeks were flushed, and I realised I hadn't responded. "Yeah," I said, toying with my spoon. "Maybe."

His chair scraped back against the tiled floor and he stood, hands white against the tabletop. "I need more than a maybe," he whispered tightly. "You know where to find me."

He left, a used spoon, half a blood orange sundae and six dollars sixty-five the only indication he'd been present.

I called him of course. His cell number hadn't changed since he'd got it in eighth grade and although it had been over a year since I'd dialled it last, I still knew the number. Deleting him as a phone contact had made surprisingly little difference when it came to deleting him from my life.

I guess I'd always known one day that it would come to this. I'd never told him that he was the reason Carly and I weren't friends anymore, because she loathed him in the special and precise way of the weak fearing the powerful, and because I had always defended him. Right up until Jenna Thomson's head had splattered on the pavement, anyway.

I'd known what he was, of course. And I'd never denied it to Carly, either. I just didn't agree that it made him a monster. Now, as I stared at my reflection in the bathroom mirror, eyes a little too wide and fingers a little too white as they clutched the phone, I had to wonder if that was only because I was a monster too.

He picked up on the fifth ring. "Yeah?"

Was I imagining it, or did my eyes turn a little green? "I'll do it," I said. I held my breath, waiting for an answer, and when I ran out of air I gulped it in greedily, like maybe oxygen was rationed for people who did evil.

"Okay," he said, and when he spoke, it was like icy water crashing down over my head, like nerves or excitement or dread. "Meet me on the corner of Raeburn and Fifth. You know the place."

I did. I just hadn't expected to go there ever again. "Now?" I said, ignoring the way my voice went squeaky around the edges, and hoping that he would too.

"Why not?" I heard the inward rush of air as he opened his mouth to say something else, but nothing came.

"What?" I said, the rough scratch on the phone's casing where I'd dropped it a week ago jagging my skin. "What is it?"

Another deep breath. "Now," with finality. "The less time you have to think about it, the better. Trust me."

I didn't ask why. I didn't need to.

"We're not going to splatter her on the concrete though, right?" I asked from my vantage point in the lowest fork of the old oak, voice barely shaking at all.

Ryan paused mid-circle to cut me a filthy look. "That's right, bring that back up again why don't you. Anything else you'd like to say, while we're on the topic?"

I shifted on my perch. "Well I was just checking!"

He sniffed, shaking his head and resuming the circle he was drawing on the path, blue chalk streaking his fingers. He completed it and stepped back, scuffed some out and redrew it to make it more circular, then surveyed it again. "I *have* been learning," he said, not looking up.

I stared at him. "Ryan, it's okay. I trust you."

He glanced up, surprised written in his eyes. Maybe he really didn't know that I'd defended him.

I shrugged. "What now?"

He pointed to a small wooden bowl he'd placed in the circle. "Ideally we'd get a hair or an eyelash or something, and put it in the bowl to anchor the spell. But we can also just write her name. That usually works okay."

I pulled out the tiny notebook I kept in my jacket pocket for emergencies, along with a miniature pen. "This do?"

Ryan nodded, and I scrawled out Carly's name in a pretty cursive font I'd learned from my grandmother. Funnily enough, I don't think she would have disapproved of it being used to curse someone. I got the feeling that she'd have been cursing people left, right and centre, if only she'd known how. I slipped from the tree and folded the paper in half before handing it to Ryan.

He stretched over the circle and dropped it into the bowl, then wiped his fingers on his shirt as though the paper had stained him.

"What now?" I asked.

"Go back to the tree." His jaw was tight and strained, and I thought about asking whether he was okay, whether he was up for this, but instead I shrugged and climbed back up to my perch.

Ryan began to shuffle around the circle, mumbling under his breath. For two full circuits, nothing happened except that his voice grew louder. He started the third circuit. Magic rose like mist from the circumference of the circle, wispy blue and red, rising up to about three feet before spiralling in to meet over the centre. Ryan shouted the final word, and gold streaked up from the bowl to meet the fog, the paper fluttering, shivering, then bursting into ash. The lights spiralled upwards, half a foot thick, three quarters, a full foot across, taller and taller until it stretched half the height of the giant, old oak.

My fingers knotted around a fistful of oak leaves.

The magic swirled and swivelled, catching its bearings. Then it swooped—straight at me.

My eyes widened and panic clawed at my chest as I remembered the one little secret I'd never told him, the thing that had never seemed important because I'd only been a baby, too young for it ever to have mattered: my name was Carly, too. But my parents, my adoptive parents who'd had me since I was three months old, had called me by my middle name—Joanna—because Carly, the other Carly, the bigger, brighter, better Carly, had been there first.

Magic engulfed me and I thrashed. *I'm not the one you want! It's not me!*

But the magic didn't listen. It bound me tighter and tighter; no matter how hard I struggled, I stayed stuck fast.

Then Ryan was there, eyes like ghosts as he squeezed my unresponsive shoulders. "I'll fix it," he said grimly. "I'll fix it. I swear."

THE UNICORN'S GIFT

Amy Laurens

"I'M SORRY," THE DOCTOR said softly as we stood in the hallway outside my apartment. "There's nothing else I can try. Nothing's working any more. Your only chance is one of *them*."

My throat tightened and my fingers fisted at my sides. I nodded. "Thanks," I said. "For trying."

He gave a curt nod by way of farewell and headed for the stairs—up, not down; clearly he had other patients to attend to in the building.

I let myself back into my apartment and bowed my head against the closed door, allowing despair and exhaustion to flood over me for a slow count of ten. At ten, I straightened, shook myself off, and headed to Gabrielle's room. "Hey," I said from the doorway when I saw she was awake.

She twitched her lips, approximating a smile. "Hey." Her dark face stood out against the pale lemon pillows, hair frizzing around it in an untamed mess. I needed to wash it. Maybe she'd let me cornrow it later on. "Any news?"

I shook my head. "Nothing works any more. The 'corns have destroyed it all."

She bit her lip fretfully and looked up at me, eyes wide.

"It's okay," I said, hurrying to perch awkwardly next to her. "We'll find one. I'll take you to one if it kills me."

Gabrielle's wide-eyed stare became a hard-edged glare. "No, you won't. Don't say stupid things like that."

I sagged. "I know. I'm sorry. You know what I mean."

She nodded.

"Tomorrow then," I said, patting her hand. "We'll try first thing. I'll fix this. I promise, I'll fix this."

Gabrielle closed her eyes, and I stroked her fingers until she fell asleep.

⁓⁓⁓

As it turned out, moving Gabrielle was impossible anyway; she was in too much pain to tolerate me bumping and bashing her about, even though I tried to be as gentle as I could. In the end, I stood back, looked at her with grief squeezing blood from my heart, and told her I'd go alone. It was a measure of how desperate she was—we both were—that she agreed without a fuss. I organized one of the few remaining neighbours to check in on her each day, left food within her reach, and set off.

From the outside, our building looked even worse. The buildings in this part of town hadn't been that great to begin with, concrete crumbling at the corners and paint flaking off in layers, but now they looked downright demolition-worthy. And there hadn't even been many 'corns in our district.

At least that meant we still had a steady water supply, and the food we'd all frantically stockpiled in the first few days of the disaster hadn't suddenly perished.

But on the other hand, it meant I had no clue where to start looking for one for Gabrielle.

It occurred to me as I reached the outskirts of our area that I'd underestimated the damage the 'corns had done to the rest of the city. All around   me, chaos rippled like an alligator's pond. Everything concrete was decaying, crumbling, melting—or just strewn in chunks all over the ground, exposing wood or metal beams where walls had once   stood. Sidewalks   had   cracked   and   crumbled, overtaken by tufts of knee-high grass and weeds as tall as my hip. The roads hadn't faired much better, asphalt split and gaping, cars scattered hither and thither like they'd been abandoned by a giant toddler—or a tornado. Most of them were rusting out, plastic dashes melted into garish shapes, synthetic upholstery already nearly weathered away.

Someone honked behind me and I glanced back in surprise. A little Greenstar, one of those new-fangled solar-powered cars that couldn't top more than thirty but were supposed to be totally green. Figures they'd be able to survive, although as it wove its way closer I noted it no longer had its original plastic dash, and the seats had been replaced with bare wood benches.

The driver, an older lady probably in her sixties, pulled the car up beside me and wound down her window. "Need a lift?"

I shrugged. "Got no money. No goods for trading." I held out my hands, indicating that all I had was what she saw.

She smiled, a warm fuzzy thing that seemed far too genuine for the circumstances. "I'm Frankie. Come on, I'll give you a lift."

"Jayla," I said, nodding. "Thank you."

⌁⌁⌁⌁

It turned out Frankie had been a nurse, back in the days before, just a year or two away from retirement. She'd spent the weeks since the 'corns had arrived driving up and down any passable roads she could find, helping out as she could. She was more than happy to drop me off in the centre of town, waving me farewell and wishing me luck. "You'll need it, Ducky," she said as she shoved the car back into gear and reversed away. "They don't grant wishes."

I knew that all too well.

The centre of town was, contrary to expectation, quiet as a rural meadow—or a graveyard. It gave a decent impression of either, knee-high grass rippling through the square in an unbroken blanket of green, building rubble sticking up at odd angles, headstones laid by a drunken mortician.

For twenty, thirty, forty minutes I walked, through ways that used to bustle and hustle but now only rustled in the breeze. My hopes fell with my shoulders and stomach. I sat on a stray boulder that looked suspiciously like it had once been a granite head and considered my options: continue on my probably-futile quest for a 'corn indefinitely, or head home empty-handed and concede defeat to Death.

A shout off to my right drew my attention: a short, black-haired fellow came running into view, waving his hands frantically. "Make way!" he shouted. "Move out of the way!"

I jumped to my feet, staring at him.

"Move!" he shouted again, hands flapping.

"Where?" I called back, gesturing at the lack of cover around.

"Anywhere!"

An instant later, I realised why: not one, not even two,

but a small herd of glorious 'corns burst into view, long white limbs stretching, pastel manes and tails flying like streamers, sharp-tipped silver horns glinting in the cold sunlight. Adrenalin shot through my body. I scooted behind some nearby rubble and slammed my back against it. I squeezed my eyes shut and prayed for sanity as the herd thundered past.

Hoof beats began to die away and I let out a cautious breath. It appeared I'd escaped unscathed. I dared a peek over the rubble mound and froze, a scream in my throat. In the second it took to convince my body to work again I realised what I was seeing: not a second herd as I'd feared, but a single, lavender-maned creature being driven by three or four men on horseback. I ducked back behind my rubble pile, took a few steadying breaths, and peeked out again.

The 'corn frothed at the mouth, saliva a pale purple that matched its mane and tail. Patches of its cloud-white fur had worn thin on its flanks, and a silvery-steel liquid seeped through. And although the 'corn still ran, it stumbled and staggered, not at all surefooted like its cousins.

One of the men on regular-horseback threw something at the flagging 'corn. It hit the 'corn's rump and exploded in a puff of dark green powder. The 'corn screamed and bucked, gathering itself up as though to try for greater speed. Instead, it tripped and fell.

As it slammed chest-first into the ground, I realised I was running towards it, and skidded to a stop. The hunters were closing in, the 'corn screaming furiously, but I didn't dare move. I couldn't. Everyone knew the stories: 'corns hurt more than they helped, and through their rabid mission to 'purify' the world they were utterly destroying it. If I went close to it while it was angry and hurting, who knew what it might do.

The hunters launched another powder puff. It exploded

over the unicorn's withers; the unicorn screamed. I clapped my hands over my ears and winced at the agony. It tore at my chest and for a moment I couldn't tell if the agony was mine or the 'corn's.

I couldn't let it suffer like that alone. I darted forward, sprinting hard to make it to the 'corn before the hunters dismounted. "No!" I threw myself in front of them just as they launched a third powder puff. It hit my shoulder and burst. I cringed, expecting pain, but instead was enveloped in a spicy, herby smell. I frowned at the green mark, confused.

Behind me, the 'corn screamed again and I whirled towards it, ignoring the hunters striding towards me with murder in their eyes. I dropped to my knees by the unicorn's head. "I'm sorry," I said. "Can I do anything?"

A rough hand grabbed me by the shoulder. "What in blazes do you think you're doing?" The man spun me around to face him.

"You're hurting it!" I said.

"Of course we're hurting it! It's a bloody unicorn!"

I glanced around at the creature writhing on the ground. "I know. I know it is." I tugged at my hair and shot the hunter a desperate glance. "Just... give me one second with it, will you?"

He shrugged and tossed a powder puff in his hand. "Your funeral. You got sixty seconds before I lob this at its nose. That'll finish it off, and you don't want to be within blasting range when that happens. You seen what the 'corns do when they're happy?"

I nodded, remembering the first time I'd seen one parading down the street, radiating light that cleansed everything in its reach. It sounded great in theory: magical unicorns that appeared out of nowhere, cleansing and purifying the world. The problem was, their definition of clean and pure was pretty darn strict. Synthetics? Gone, and that included building materials, clothing, food—and medicines. Sure, disease and sickness was also purified, but there's a difference between a cancerous tumour suddenly disappearing, and whole chunks of 'faulty' DNA being ripped from someone's cells. The former you could survive; the latter not so much.

"So you can imagine what will happen when one dies, then." He stared me down.

I stared back, determined.

The hunter nodded. "One minute."

I knelt by the unicorn's face as the hunter retreated to talk with his partners. It whinnied softly and I reached out, fingers trembling. I hesitated right before I touched it. "What are you going to do to me?" I asked, uncertain why I felt so much sympathy for this creature of destruction as it died. Maybe that was part of the 'corn's power, luring me in on its deathbed. Maybe it was hope.

I let my fingertips rest against its cheek, pure white hair impossibly soft, like down, or superfine velvet. Heat seared my fingers as energy shot up through my arms and into the base of my skull. Waves of colour and sound shot through my mind, hot, cold, loud, soft, crimson, magenta, viridian, gold. I tried to pull back, but the current of energy held me tight. It poured into me, filling my fingers and toes, hands and feet, wrists, ankles, legs, arms...

Warmth suffused me and lifted me to my feet, off the ground, and spun me gently, scribing a golden circle in the air. I couldn't tell if the warmth was pleasant or if it hurt; it straddled that strange boundary between pleasure and pain and all I could do was try to breathe through it.

With a sudden burst, the connection severed and I dropped to the ground. I blinked, disoriented, then realised the dark shape in front of me was the hunter, standing over the unicorn's body as dark green powder dispersed into the air. "Ow."

The hunter glanced at me. "You okay?"

I looked down at my arms. A frisson of fear travelled through me as I realised my arms were glowing. I stretched, wriggled my fingers, and looked back at the hunter. "Yeah. I think so."

Another man laughed behind me. "We thought you were a gonner for sure." He clapped me heartily on the shoulder. Energy sizzled through me and stung his hand. He snatched it back and stared. "What the hell?"

I looked at my fingers again and wriggled them. Energy sparked from fingertip to fingertip. I met the second man's eye and smiled. "Your skin. It's perfect."

He lifted his hands to his face and dragged his fingers slowly down his cheeks, eyes wide. "You," he said.

I didn't give him the chance to finish. Who knew what that powder might do to me now? All I knew was that I had to get home. I might not be able to take Gabrielle to a unicorn, or take one to her, but this? This I could take home. I laughed into the wind as I ran. "Hold on, Gabbi. I'm coming."

⌇⌇⌇⌁⌁⌁⌁⌇⌇⌇

SHADOWS
Amy Laurens

CRACKPOTS AND STALKERS

It's the shadows that tell you someone really is, much more than what they look like or even how they act. People can train themselves to cover up anything; but the shadows never lie. Of course, I couldn't always see the shadows. It took my own shift to realise how. But once I knew, I could never go back to how I had been—even if it meant I had to live with my own shadow.

CANDANCE RAN DOWN THE street, brown hair slicked back in a ponytail, sweat sheening her forehead and dripping down her cleavage. The late evening sun melted over the street, turning everything honey-coloured, and everyone else seemed to react by becoming slow themselves, like the light had turned viscous. Candance alone sped through the evening, keen to get her jog over and done with so she could hit the shower and get ready for dinner.

Usually, jogging was enough to let her zone out and forget the worries of the day; this evening, not so much. Flashes of deep blue satin, glimmerings of diamonds and the faint rush of applause intruded on her quiet, threatening to steal her concentration away entirely.

Frustrated, Candance ground her teeth and pounded harder against the pavement. *I will not be distracted*, she told herself. *I will not be distracted.*

The conflicting scents of hot tar, exhaust fumes, and freshly cut grass mingled in the air, and she breathed deeply, counting out her strides as she did. In-one-two-three, out-one-two-three, and on and on down the street until formal dinners faded from mind and she forgot about everything except her feet hitting the concrete, her arms pumping at her sides and the steady rhythm of her breaths.

She turned the final corner for home feeling more centred than she'd managed all week—and cried out as she ran into a person standing hunched in the middle of the path. A crack in the pavement seemed to leap up and tangle itself around her toes, and before she knew it, Candance's palms scraped the ground, quickly followed by her knees.

Hissing, she lifted her hands to survey the damage. Fine gravel had embedded in her skin and the heels of her palms bled. Her knees weren't much better. Wincing, she struggled to her feet. *Well, this is going to look amazing with my gown*, she thought, and pursed her lips.

"You shouldn't go, you know," said a voice, and Candance whirled to face the stranger. A woman, though her voice had been deep enough to belong to a man, old but not frail, hunched but not weakened.

"Go where?"

"To the dinner tonight."

Candance's heart leapt in her chest. "How do you know about the dinner?"

The woman simply shrugged. "Don't go."

Heart pounding now with adrenalin as well as exertion, Candance licked her lips. "That's none of your business." She turned away.

"Suit yourself," said the woman. "Most people prefer not to have an audience is all. Don't say I didn't warn you."

Candance stopped, struggling. On the one hand, the woman was obviously a crackpot at best, and a stalker at worst. On the other... "Why not?" she said at last, back still to the woman.

"You haven't felt it waking?" the woman asked in apparent surprise.

"Felt what?" Irritation blossomed. Stupid woman, standing around where people could run into her, making vague prognostications and being obtuse. *Why am I even still listening?* Candance snapped to herself.

"You truly do not know what you are?" The woman shuffled into Candance's peripheral vision and peered at her. "How strange."

What I am? Candance shuddered, squashing the fear that was trying to take root in the back of her mind. "I have no idea what you're talking about. I'm leaving now." She launched back into a jog, wondering why she'd even felt the need to respond. She should have just ignored the woman from the start, kept jogging and not listened to a thing. She glanced back over her shoulder, pulse skipping when she accidentally made eye contact with the woman.

"Don't go," the woman called again. "It's waking. I can see your shadow, even if you can't."

Candance's gaze flicked down to her shadow in front of her. She frowned. It was a perfectly average shadow, and she could see it perfectly well. What on earth...? And even more strange, when she glanced back again, curious despite herself, the woman had gone.

Oh well, Candance thought, rolling her neck as she ran. *Don't think about it. Pretend it didn't happen.* She shoved aside the uneasiness and told herself it was only nerves.

QUICKENING

The thing about pretending is that we all do it. We all pretend to be something we're not, and we do it most of the time without even thinking. And yet the very first thing we look for in a mate is someone we don't have to pretend with, someone we can be our deepest, realest selves around.

I sometimes wonder what the world would be like if we all just stopped pretending. Then I remember the shadows, and know: sometimes, the only thing standing between civilisation and anarchy is our willingness to pretend.

Candance smoothed the final hairpin into place and surveyed the result in the mirror. A triple strand of diamantes encircled her neck and another circled one wrist; genuine diamond-encrusted hairpins accented her updo. The midnight satin gown glimmered softly under the lights of her bathroom and she allowed her lips to quirk up slightly at the corners. She scrubbed up okay.

She headed back through the bedroom, snagging shoes on the way, and paused in the front entryway to slip them on just as someone knocked at the door. "Coming," she called as she did up the final buckle and tottered to the door.

"Allen, hi," she said as he grinned and proffered a cream rose in full bloom. She tapped the front of her left shoulder and leaned forward as Allen pinned it onto her dress.

"Stunning," he pronounced, and offered her his arm.

Grinning in return, Candance took it and allowed him to lead her toward the car. Allen had taken her under his wing five years ago when she'd first arrived in town. They'd hit it off right away, in a friendly, brother-sister sort of way, and Candance hadn't been at all surprised when he'd first introduced her to his boyfriend. Five years later, Allen and she were better friends than ever, and he'd been the easy choice for an escort to this evening's do, where any other invitation might be seen as a serious proposal on her behalf, and turning up alone was impermissible.

Candance paused as Allen stooped to open the car, all prepared to flash him a charming smile and slide into the front seat; instead, she frowned as something unfamiliar surged through her stomach. It almost felt like the lurch of adrenalin, only it was hotter, quicker, there-and-then-gone.

"Are you okay?"

Candance pretended she'd just been smoothing down her skirt. "Of course." She gave him the planned smile and climbed into the car, stiffening as the strange sensation seized her again.

Allen closed her door and rounded the front of the car to climb into the driver's seat. "All set?" he asked, looking her up and down. His eyes lingered over her stomach and his lips tightened into the barest suggestion of a frown. "Are you sure you want to go tonight?"

Candance knitted her brows. "Of course I am. I have to go. I *want* to go. I—" She cut off and hissed as the feeling surged again, this time with a hot edge of pain.

Allen raised an eyebrow and glanced pointedly at Candance's hands, which now clutched her belly. "It's all under control?"

"Of course." She'd eaten something funny, or maybe overdone the run, that was all. It was nothing. She'd be fine.

"So, tell me about the fabulous speech you'll be making tonight," Allen said, turning the key in the ignition and pulling smoothly out into the street.

Candance leaned back and closed her eyes. A feeling of well-practiced calm soothed over her and she smiled, anticipating the moment. "I can't believe they chose me."

Allen laughed. "Probably not the best way to begin."

She laughed with him. "No, probably not." Still, it was the truth: she'd been surprised enough when her boss had told her that she'd been nominated for the prestigious ATS Santo Award for her research into the social behaviour of oceanic bearded dragons. The news that she'd won had been almost beyond belief.

Candance gasped as her stomach contracted. She tightened her fingers convulsively and Allen shot her a worried glance. She smiled back at him. "I'll start with the story about the dragon biting my finger when I was in Hawaii that time." *Please ignore it,* she begged him with her eyes. Tonight, of all nights, everything had to be perfect. She'd worked so hard... Her aunt's voice rang in her ears, reminding her that of all the people who'd tried to make a name for themselves in marine herpetology, only three were currently making a job of it.

Allen nodded and focused on the road ahead, worry still tightening the corners of his mouth and eyes—but at least he'd let it go for now.

Candance knotted her fingers in her lap. "Then," she continued, ignoring the tremors in her belly that felt like her last meal was trying to escape, "after they're all dying of laughter at me, I'll turn on the serious-face charm," she tested it out on Allen, eyes wide and serious, "and they'll love me. Right?"

He reached out and lightly punched her shoulder. "They'll adore you."

Twenty minutes later they pulled up outside the Princeton Hotel, a giant, fifty-storey affair spangled in gold and purple lighting and backdropped by the Bellington Wharf, home to all boats worth more than Candance's house. Candance popped the passenger door open and stretched one leg out. Cramps hit her in the stomach like knives, and she doubled over.

Allen grabbed her wrist and turned her, searching her face. "You don't have to do this," he said. "Not tonight."

Candance glanced up to where her boss stood waiting at the top of the stairs, and heard her aunt once again. "Yes," she said, straightening, teeth gritted as she forced away the pain. "I do."

"Candance, you can walk away from this. We can leave—"

She shook her head. "I can't do that to them."

"Sure you can, we just—"

"Look, I'm going, alright?" she snapped as another wave of nausea flooded over her. Nausea was better than pain. She exhaled. "Sorry. I'm going. They're expecting me, this is a big deal, and I can't just walk away. I won't," she added.

Candance stared across at Allen and put a hand on his shoulder. "I appreciate your concern," she said, softly now. "But if I leave, it's not just the ceremony I'm walking away from. It's the Award, my job... everything." Tears welled in her eyes. "I can't just walk away."

"Okay," he replied just as softly. He squeezed her arm. "You can do this."

Candance nodded and swiped away the tear.

"Go get 'em, tiger." Allen grinned. "I'll meet you in there shortly."

Candance watched him drive away towards the car park, then turned to face the hotel, stomach flipping from nausea—and nerves.

THE BEAST WITHIN

I often wish I'd listened to Allen, that night. But then I wonder what would have happened if I had. I might still have my job, for one thing. And the Award. That was what hit me hardest afterwards— Aunt Clarisse had been right. My chosen career path was a complete dead end.

She was wrong about the rest, though. I wouldn't go back for the world.

"And now," said the presenter on stage while the lights glimmered off his perfectly coiffed hair, "the winner of the ATS Santo Award, Candance Murray!"

The crowd erupted into applause like a flight of gem-toned butterflies. Candance pushed her chair back and stood, demurring as Allen offered his arm and her table companions offered their congratulations. Her stomach fluttered and Candance smoothed her hands over her belly as she glided up to the front.

The first two steps proved no obstacle, but on the third, while the crowd still cheered behind her, the same stabbing pain from the car ripped through Candance's gut, and she stumbled. A few members of the crowd gasped as Candance struggled to right herself, the floor swimming before her eyes.

No, she told herself. *Come on. Get up there and thank them. You can't fall apart now.*

Candance forced herself upright, clinging to the narrow handrail. Gritting her teeth, she conquered the final two steps and strode to the podium, her shadow dancing under her feet, flung every way by the multi-directional lighting.

The walk to the podium took years, and by the time she reached it, the applause had well and truly died. Candance's cheeks felt burningly hot, and as she clutched at the podium for support she wished the presenter would just hold the stupid trophy still so she could claim it. And why did he have to wave it about in that ridiculous manner anyway?

He leaned towards her. "Are you okay?"

"Of course I'm okay," Candance snapped, reaching for the award. "Give me that."

He frowned, but passed the slab of glass on its wooden mount to her and guided her to the microphone. "Candance Murray!" he said again, and the room broke into over-enthusiastic applause underscored by a riot of whispers.

Candance swallowed, wetting her throat, and opened her mouth. Instead of the thank you she'd intended, she groaned as another bout of pain stabbed through her. Over the podium, her shadow flickered. Candance stared. She really must be unwell; for a moment it had looked like she'd grown a snout. She shook her head and tried again. "Thank you," she said. Her voice sounded gravelly and raw. "It's an honour to... receive..." She tried to remember what the award was called.

Allen rose from their table and started towards her, weaving between chairs, eyes fixed on her. Candance smiled. Sweet of him to come help her with her speech. She didn't need help, though; she was doing just fine. Why, the entire audience was holding their collective breath, just waiting to see what she'd say next! She grinned at them, then blinked in surprise at the slab of glass in her hand. She frowned. "What's this?"

The presenter stretched his lips, but Candance could tell that he was unhappy. Something about the eyes and the way that he tried to usher her away from the podium. Probably it was this stupid glass thing they'd given her.

The nausea in her stomach was making it hard to think, but really, who in their right mind would have made such an ugly, misshapen lump?

Allen reached the bottom of the podium and hissed out her name. "Candance! Come down here!"

The presenter pushed her towards Allen, so she took one hesitant step, then another. Allen smiled encouragingly. "That's right, just keep coming."

Halfway to him, Candance gagged and retched as something tried to claw its way through her stomach. The award dropped to the floor with a heavy thud, and Candance followed.

Allen's arms wrapped around her and he shoved something at her mouth. "Swallow this," he whispered urgently. "Now!"

Candance gulped the sticky paste down, then gagged again as Allen hauled her to her feet.

"No," Allen said, brushing the presenter aside. "I'll just take her out for some fresh air. I'm sure she'll be fine. You just carry on," he added when the presenter looked lost.

"No," Candance gasped as she stubbed her foot on the award and it rolled away. "No, I need that." She couldn't quite remember why, but the burning need was there.

"We're a bit past that, don't you think?" Allen muttered as he steered her by the elbow towards the nearest exit. "Just get out of here. I don't know what on earth you were thinking, coming tonight. I should never have let you leave the house."

Abruptly Candance realised that her cheeks were cold because they were now outside; the wind was cooling tears on her face. "No," she whispered.

Pain wracked through her body again, and for an instant her shadow flickered, something huge and toothy and clawed.

For just that instant, Candance reeled in shock; she knew what was trying to claw its way out of her stomach. Eyes wide, terror slicking her palms, Candance turned to Allen. "What's happening to me?"

Allen stopped short and stared at her. "What do you mean?"

She trembled. "Allen, I feel like... like something is trying to rip my stomach out." And like I'm about a hairsbreadth away from turning into a monster. "What's—" Her words were lost in a growl as her teeth flashed, long and needle sharp, and her body billowed to something twelve feet tall and scaly before plummeting her back into her own skin.

Candance reeled.

Allen caught her arm and steadied her before leading her out towards the farthest wharf. "Here," he said as they paused where the paving met wooden slats. "Eat more of this. It'll help keep it under control."

"But what *is* it?" Candance said over a tongueful of the sweet, sticky paste. She swallowed and felt the beast in her stomach settle a little.

Allen heaved an almighty sigh, then stalked off down the wharf.

Candance followed. "What is it?" she asked, unable to sort the fluttering and palpitating into neat categories of sick and nerves and beast. "What's wrong with me?"

Allen sighed again and ran a hand over his head. "Nothing's wrong with you. You're changing."

"Changing?"

"Your beast," he said. "It's breaking free. You're changing. Did you see your shadow flickering before? I saw that at your house, when I gave you the rose, and knew it was coming, but I didn't expect it to be this fast." His hand ran over his hair again.

Candance clenched her teeth and glared. "What do you mean, changing? And if you knew something was wrong with me, why didn't you say something earlier, in the car?"

"I thought you knew!"

Candance cocked her head. "What, that I had a monstrous beast lurking inside of me, just waiting to break free?"

"No!" Allen threw his hands up. "That you're a theriomorph. A skin-walker. Shape-shifter. It runs in families; I assumed your parents would have prepared you."

Candance reeled, head pounding, stomach still roiling. Somewhere out in the darkness, a curlew called. "My parents died when I was eight."

"Oh."

The silence stretched again, broken only by the cries of the curlew and the lap-lap-lap of water against the wharf. *He's thinking about me*, Candance thought. *He's wondering how to tell me I've become a monster and he doesn't want to be friends anymore.* Suddenly, that seemed like the worst thing that could possibly happen, far worse than turning into a monster, or even people knowing she turned into one. 'People' was amorphous, nebulous; Allen was *Allen*.

"So," she said, aiming for casual as she leaned back against the wharf's railing and hooked her arms around it. "Other than the fact that I was clearly making a fool of myself, why whip me out here and feed me that... stuff?" Her heart hammered. "Also," she said, straightening, "how did you know to do that?"

Allen seemed to take his time thinking, turning to link his arms through the railing next to her and surveying the stars. "The paste slows the transition, makes it more controllable and less painful. It's a relatively new invention. As for the other, I could see that you were about to change, and..." He shrugged. "We never show ourselves in public."

"We?" Candance cut in. "You're one too?"

"Yes. A grey fox." He weaved his head and caught her gaze. "Are you listening to me? We *don't show ourselves*. It's safer that way. Especially for the more unusual"—he shot her a glance—"of us." He frowned. "What are you, anyway? A lizard?"

Candance smirked, eyes narrowing. She'd only had an instant to meet her inner animal, but an instant had been all she'd needed. "A lizard?" she asked cuttingly. "Really?" The change bubbled up inside again, and this time she knew it wouldn't be suppressed; it was too strong, too hot, and holding it in would scorch her from the inside out. So this time, she let it go, laughing in delight as the power swirled up from her belly, around her chest, and tingled down her arms and legs.

Suffused with the warm light of change, her fingernails shot out and claws punched the air, one quickly after the other, a staccato of rifle shots. Muscles stretched, tendons shifted and popped, and her bones lengthened and strengthened. Stability and swiftness, perfect balance and poise; her new frame simply *worked*.

And then, as easily as it had begun, the change was over, and Candance stood towering over Allen, clacking her teeth and chortling as best as she could with her new vocal cords.

Allen, to his great credit, hadn't moved an inch, though the whites of his eyes and the stench of fear sweat gave him away. "A raptor," he said, and swore. "Of course you had to be a raptor. We haven't seen a prehistoric mutation in decades, and now, just as we're getting the whole concept under control and starting to regulate it, you show up as a *bloody raptor*."

Candance clacked her teeth again and attempted a laugh, which came out as more of a strangled roar than anything recognisably humorous—but Allen seemed to understand.

He rolled his eyes and shrugged himself away, huffing deeply. "Well, go on then. You'll have energy burning through your system like nothing else, if you're anything like normal. Go run it off somewhere people won't see you." He squeezed his eyes shut and massaged his temples. "And do me a favour, will you?"

Candance peered down at him, trying for any expression but hungry, because the finer details of emotions were beyond her at the moment. The power, the heat, the adrenalin surging through her veins and sizzling in her skin and making her want to run, and run, and run, and run...

Allen sighed resignedly. "Just come find me when you're yourself again, will you? We need to talk." He glanced up at Candance, the first look he'd given her since he'd sworn at her—and immediately, he shook his head and walked away, hands deep in his pockets.

The wind rolled in from the ocean, whipping up waves and bringing with it the promise of adventure. Candance waited until Allen was nearly back inside, let her inner beast roar—just once, quietly—and sprinted away into the night.

∿∿∿∿∿∿

PURITY
Amy Laurens

THE PARKING LOT IS covered in a foot of storm water and the wind whips waves up like it's a sea. I've no idea how the thing we're hunting got stuck in a service station—or what we'll find once we're inside.

Beside me, Reg shifts, his dark, lined face twitching and flickering like it has a life of its own. "Think we should do it?" he mutters.

I jerk my head in a nod that feels precariously like falling. "Of course we should."

He rearranges the shotgun under his trench coat and we set out.

The dark concrete of the parking lot turns the water inky grey, and oil slicks float on the surface. The water seeps into my boots, probing with icy fingers that set me shivering even through the garbage bags I'm wearing as waterproof knee-high socks. The wind cuts through my thin coat—it doesn't help that one sleeve is nearly torn off and the buttons are all missing—and all that, combined with the hunger gnawing in my stomach, is almost enough to make me wish we hadn't set out on this foolhardy quest in the first place. But sadly, when you're hunting a unicorn, there's no stopping till it's dead—or you are.

Reg trudges on, heavy steps sloshing and splashing the foul water, and I follow resignedly. All over town it's like this now: half submerged, water leeching oil and tar and carbon monoxide and other toxic chemicals from the buildings. It's only been a week, but already the southlands are crumbling; their concrete was cheap, sand-filled stuff, the bricks half-backed clay, and none of it is strong enough to withstand the onslaught.

One of Reg's splashes catches me on the cheek, and I reel for a moment as the water zaps like electricity. I wipe it off with the back of my sleeve, knowing that where it's been, my skin will be left glowing and fresh. I can totally understand why the first victims fell willingly, bathing themselves in water that seemed to create perfection.

Thank heavens I have goggles on.

The wind brings steel-coloured clouds to boil overhead, and I prod Reg in the back. "Storm's coming."

He glances up, exhales heavily, and carries on.

A downpour will be the end of us if we don't find shelter—but we're close now, touchingly close, and we couldn't break away even if we tried.

The service station looms ahead, casting a shadow even in this dim, directionless light. It's a toad hulking in the corner of its pond, waiting for a fly to mistake it for a boulder, ready to dart out its tongue and consume the unwary. Light radiates from windows that are crystal clear, dripping sludge marks below their panes the only remnants of their former dirt-and-oil film. Somewhere in there, working to purify the whole damn world, is the unicorn.

We duck under the shelter of the awning right as the rain begins. As usual, it's torrential, a flash downpour that blocks the senses: everything is grey, rushing water, the smell of wet concrete and oil.

I cock my head; underneath the roar of the water, something else is groaning. I glance up. "Look out!" I tackle Reg to the ground and roll, and the collapsing roof misses us by inches. We're stuck between the wreckage and the building now, and all I can see is the pitted, metal girders that have twisted and torn.

"You right?" I ask Reg, offering him a hand.

Muttering under his breath, he ignores me and shoves himself to his feet. He resets his bucket hat on his greying head, adjusts the shotgun, and tightens the sash of his trench coat.

Once I'm sure he's okay, I pull my own coat tighter around me and fold my arms to stop it flapping. The comforting weight of the frabah powder weighs down my pocket.

Our eyes meet. It's time to go in. With a deep inhale, I place my palms against the sparkling glass door of the service centre.

Reg stands shoulder to shoulder with me. "Go on, then, lass."

I push. Sweet, fresh air wafts out to meet us; the unicorn must have been here a while.

We ease ourselves through the door and stand staring at the aisles. Water covers the floor here too, though not as deeply, and instead of deathly grey it's brilliant, rainbow hued and swirled like a Paddle Pop of old—though of course, 'of old' is only really last month.

On the shelf next to the door, just to our right, a chip packet has survived unscathed. Halfway down the aisle in front of us, a packet of Tim Tams seems intact. I wade over to the ice cream freezer and peer in. It's a riot of colour from the plastic and the ice creams, and half-melted chocolate sludges the inside walls. The glass that covers it, though, is pristine.

I push my goggles up, wiping my hands up my face then back down over my eyes. I'm tired. This has to end. Maybe if we'd been out bush it wouldn't have mattered so much; if we didn't live in a jungle of concrete and steel, food stuffed full of artificial chemicals and preservatives, maybe then the unicorn wouldn't have mattered.

But we do, and it does. If we're purified, we'll die.

A noise sounds behind the counter. Reg and I whip around in the same instant and light, blinding, glorious, perfect light, streams out from the unicorn, burning my eyes. I throw my arms up against it and the shotgun barks beside me, once, twice, and again.

That's my cue. I dart my eyes open for an instant to check that the way is clear, and then running blind I sprint towards the counter—towards the unicorn that is our death. I wrap my hand around the pure hemp bag holding organic herbs that, crushed finely together, make frabah powder.

I can feel the unicorn's light burning me. My tatty, filthy clothes fall away, first the garbage bags, then the coat, my shirt and pants, and finally my elastane-blended sports bra. Thank heavens I'm wearing cotton undies. But I've no time to be embarrassed (and I've nothing that'll bounce anyway), because the light is burning my skin now—though at least if I come out of this alive I'll be unicorn-bathed, my skin flawless and clear.

But I'm at the counter, and I launch myself over it, scrabbling on the little shelves that once held chocolate bars. I'm kneeling on it and the unicorn, blindingly white, pure bliss, perfection incarnate, stands before me, eyeing me with one glorious golden eye before swinging its deadly point towards me. I reach into hemp bag, grab a handful of powder, and as the unicorn stabs, I toss. The powder sticks to the unicorn like glue.

It freezes, death-point half an inch from goring my stomach. My heart's pounding in my ears so loud I can't even hear the rain any more. The unicorn's glow turns gold. All over it, hairline cracks run like spiders, faster and faster and faster until—

The unicorn shatters. The chime of it sounds through the air and I cringe, hands over my ears. Sharp pain pops in my left air and my hand comes away wet with blood. Crystal shards rain down, slicing into my skin.

Something sweeps over me and I struggle wildly, but it's Reg, covering me with the coat he's stripped out of, and the noise I can hear in my good ear is just the alarm system of the building as he helps me down off the counter.

I stand beside him, shivering. The ceiling drips, rainbow water swirls around our feet, and outside the rain has stopped. Something golden bursts through the window and my heart stops for a second because it looks like the last light of the unicorn—but it's sunshine, and already the window it shines through is grimier, and the water in the parking lot's clearing.

Reg grunts and hands me that last chip packet. "Okay, lass?"

I nod, accepting it. "Okay."

THANK YOU!

Thank you so much for reading our short stories. We hope you had fun—we know we did! Don't forget you can access more of our short stories absolutely free on the *Darkness & Good* blog. You can find the story blog at http://darknessandgood.blogspot.com and we'd love to see you there!

If you enjoyed reading this anthology, please also consider leaving a review at your favourite online outlet—books live and die on reviews, and even one short comment can make a difference!

ABOUT THE AUTHORS

LIANA BROOKS once read the book *Good Omens* by Neil Gaiman and Terry Pratchett and noted that both of their biographies invited readers to send in money (or banana daiquiris). That seems to have worked well for them. Liana prefers strawberry daiquiris (virgin!) and will never say no to large amounts of cash in unmarked bills. Her books are sweet and humorous with just enough edge to keep you reading past your bedtime.

Liana is the author of the popular *Heroes and Villains* superheroes series, and the last book in her *Time And Shadows* series of time travel thrillers is also now available from Harper Collins: You can find *Decoherence* (and the first two books) anywhere good books are found!

AMY LAURENS is an Australian author of science fiction and fantasy stories for all ages. After completing a university education involving many twists and turns, through more faculties than ought reasonably to exist, Amy now spends her day as a high school English teacher. No, she is not going to do your homework for you. Not even the English bit. Sorry. Have a cookie instead.

Amy's short stories have been published in a variety of magazines and collected in anthologies such as Tyche Books' *Ride The Moon* and the SFR Brigade's *Stories From The SFR Brigade*. She has a non-fiction book on worldbuilding, *From The Ground Up*, forthcoming in 2019.